Calypso, Dreaming

Calypso Dreaming

CHARLES BUTLER

An imprint of HarperCollins*Publishers*

First published in Great Britain by CollinsVoyager 2002
CollinsVoyager is an imprint of HarperCollins*Publishers* Ltd
77-85 Fulham Palace Road, Hammersmith,
London, W6 8JB

The HarperCollins website address is:
www.**fire**and**water**.com

1 3 5 7 9 8 6 4 2

ISBN 0 00 712856 8

Printed and bound in Great Britain by
Omnia Books Limited, Glasgow

Contents

To Stephen, Ute, Æfleda,
Wulfric and Dunstan,
who made a go of it.

PART ONE

THE GOD-BOTHERERS

1. Sweetholm

"Sweetholm! Do you remember it?"

Tansy peered through the telescope. In its depths a piece of clockwork was counting out their time and turning it to cash. The island bobbed up against the glass. It was low and flat, but for the abrupt brown hill at the western tip.

"Of course she doesn't remember, Geoff," said Tansy's mother. "She was hardly walking when she came last."

"You'd be surprised what sticks sometimes. Even at that age."

Tansy opened her mouth to reply, then clapped it shut again. Dad was wrong, of course. Of course and as usual. But she didn't need to say it. Not today, when everything ought to be perfect.

"I remember it from the photos Uncle John sent. It looks closer than I imagined, though. Is it really five miles out? I can see buildings."

"Five miles by ferry," said her father. "But that's going from Plinth. And the ferry's got shoals to negotiate, remember. Tricky waters." He gestured to where the water was stippled with dark patches. "As the gull flies, we're closer here on the headland. Of which, as you can see, Sweetholm is geologically an extension – and Longholm beyond it."

Geoff unfolded the map on his knee, standing like a flamingo with something to prove as a thermal billowed up and ballooned the paper.

"It's not that we don't believe you, Dad," said Tansy, turning back to the car.

Their car was parked in the small semicircle of gravel at the head of the Down. A lane ran back, dividing one bleating field from another. It led into the main road down to Plinth. There were two cars parked there, their own and a black Volkswagen in which an elderly couple were eating sandwiches under the late June sun.

Geoff ignored the retreat to the car and put another coin in the slot. He moved the telescope over to the next bay along their own coast, and the harbour town of Plinth. Every day in summer a ferry set sail from there to Sweetholm, with a cargo of ornithologists, hermits and trippers, though Sweetholm was just too far away to make a day trip comfortable. That was where the beauty of the place lay – in its splendid near-isolation. Then he noticed the time and that the ferry was already docked.

But in such a place hurry was impossible. With the telescope still whirring, Geoff climbed into the car then inched it to the road and let it drop, braking all the time, down the steep, ear-popping hill into town. It was eleven in the morning and some of the shops were only just opening. One man, unlocking the door of his picture gallery, glanced at the car as it parked beside the ferry offices and shook his head with an air of frank reproof. Geoff looked out instinctively for No Parking signs, but found none. Perhaps they just looked disreputable in the unwashed Volvo.

Tansy and her mother waited as Geoff dealt with the ticket side of things. Her mother seemed exhausted, with her head on her hand, her hand propped on an elbow, her elbow wedged into the car door. It seemed as if she were thinking of something else, or of somewhere she would rather be than here, teetering on the brink of an adventure.

The ferry was the open-air kind, with room for four vehicles at most. The mate hauled boxes of supplies into the dark hold. Even before she was out of the car, Tansy noticed the boat's slight movement and the slapping of the water against its sides. But there was no wind to speak of as they descended to the deck. Then the ropes were cast, the water churned and they had left Britain behind.

Tansy's parents stood on either side of the ferry, having settled into a mutual sulk. They had their backs to each other, like a pair of novelty bookends. The female bookend was a bit queasy: Hilary had never been good with water. The other passengers had drifted into groups. Three men with backpacks made their way to the bows and stood, eyes shielded, to catch the white wing of a seabird flashing fifty yards out on the tinselled water.

"Isn't that a Mediterranean gull?"

"Yes, look!" Tansy heard them exclaim with quiet excitement. "This far north!"

The gulls all looked the same to Tansy. She supposed birdwatchers would be migrating daily to the island. Meanwhile, another group of passengers was chatting with the captain, whom they clearly knew. Locals, she guessed, wanting to distinguish themselves from the tourists with whom they shared the boat. She remembered what her mother had said about the islanders: "They'll never let us in, Geoff. They'll talk to their sheep more than they will to us. And you expect us to house-sit here all summer?"

"Well, John's made a go of it and he's no more an islander than I am. You do come out with the most awful prejudices, Hilary," said Geoff. "You never used to be so cynical."

"I speak as I find. As I *have* found."

To which there was no answer – except the gabble of the water turned by the ferry's prow and the wash pushed out behind it. Tansy stared down at her palms. All at once she felt immensely old, older by far than her parents. As old, possibly, as the limestone pebble scuffing the boards at her feet. She looked south to Plinth, now fast receding, and welcomed the invisibility offered by distance. A curse couldn't follow them across the water, could it? Those experiments with Kate Quilley, the Cursing Candle and the rest – surely the sea would wash the memory of their magic from her? But she was not easy until they had rounded the rocky islet of Longholm and seen its sleek, unreflecting blackness ooze up between them and the village.

The only other passenger was a young man, tanned and lean with several days' black stubble. He had spent half the journey sitting at the wheel of his old white camper van before stepping unsteadily on to the deck. He was looking at his watch now. Like Hilary he seemed impatient for their journey to be over, but not because of seasickness. More as if he had an appointment on Sweetholm that he dared not break. There was nothing in him of holiday excitement, no curiosity to see the Longholm seals, which the captain was bringing to their attention. The camper van, now Tansy looked at it, was actually a converted ambulance. You could see the words underneath the paint job, ghosting through: *Wessex Health Authority*. At the front someone had once painted 'AMBIENCE' in backward letters, but now that lame joke too was censored with white paint.

There were grey seals on Longholm. The captain had brought the boat about, to give their cameras time. He stood there sucking at his pipe, while the tourists crowded to the side of the boat to watch the great, clumsy-sleek lumberers rear their heads or slide down the rocks to reappear as a black, inquisitive dome, no more than a shadow in the waves' cup of shadows.

The young man hung back a little, as did the Sweetholm locals, who had seen it all before. Not for them the undignified jostle to the side of the ferry. But with him it was not disdain.

Tansy found herself wondering if he was superstitious about being snapped by the cameras. Or perhaps it was the domed heads of the seals themselves he found repugnant.

Geoff had taken Hilary by the arm. "What's wrong? Why won't you tell me?"

"Nothing's wrong." The arm wriggled free. "I just want to be off this boat. Can't you see I'm ill?"

"Then take a nip of this at least." Geoff had a hip flask in his hand.

"Why aren't we *moving*?" asked Hilary, almost shouting. She turned to the captain. "Are you going to take us to Sweetholm or do we have to wait for a tow from one of these wretched seals?"

The captain gave her a slow, wide grin. He was charmed.

"Aren't you even going to answer me?"

Laboriously, the captain consulted his watch. "We always come about at Longholm Point. People like to see the seals."

"They've seen them now, so *please* let's get on."

Still with the same grin the captain turned to the controls and pushed a lever forward. The engine hubbubed, and the ferry turned through a foaming circle of water and progressed unhurriedly to its destination on the far side of Sweetholm.

The Haven was the island's one harbour. Elsewhere, the land plummeted in stark cliffs or was skirted with lavish margins of mud. The undredged quicksands were an asylum for wading birds. The sand and mud squirmed with life, but had also sucked down sheep, dogs, even (the guidebook said) occasional unwary humans. A party of Edwardian nuns had made their last pilgrimage to the site of St Brigan's ancient chapel and been swallowed, a hundred years before.

In the Haven a broad shingle beach lashed back the seafront. The land stuck a long jaw seaward, just beneath the water's surface. The rocks allowed only one route to the jetty, a maze in which the jetty seemed at first to be almost overshot, then curled back upon, sidled up to almost, and surprised by the sudden weight of a ferry upon it. Water gushed out to counter the land's push. Lorry tyres strapped to the jetty cushioned the stone wall behind. No one awaited them.

Now the nimble mate leapt out to moor the ferry and a hydraulic switch lowered the ramp over which the meagre island traffic was to roll. The cyclists first, and the young man in his camper van, which spluttered a little as it took the one asphalt road on Sweetholm uphill and past the patchwork of shopfronts, the cottage gardens and the harbour master's house. Past Sweetholm Post Office too, where you could get your card stamped with a date-marked puffin and sent back to the mainland by the same boat. This, for the next three months, was to be their home.

"Where's Uncle John's place?" asked Tansy, peering along the sea front.

"Inland, up behind the village. You can't see it from here."

The Haven buildings had a huddled look, precarious between wind and ocean. Even on a summer day like this, with the breeze no more than a slight shifting of the light on the whitewashed cottage walls, Tansy was glad to be climbing to the moor above the Haven, beyond reach of the sea's white fingers. There was no one to be seen behind the green rail above the beach, but a lad in jeans and a cap was fiddling with a bale of netting nearby.

It was quiet here, an odd reflection of unpeopled Plinth, so near, so far away beyond Longholm. Not quiet in the Plinth way, though. This was a busy quiet, almost a furtive one. Somewhere, in those pretty cottages or up on the unseen inland moor, a tremendous subject was claiming the island's attention. The Haven was a face in which only the eye-whites showed.

"Tansy, are you coming?" called Hilary. She and Geoff had

already strapped themselves in, both anxious to get the journey done at last. What waited for them at the end of it would decide their summer happiness. And that might decide their whole lives together. It didn't make for relaxation.

2. Crusoe's Castle

Geoff had made most of the running, Tansy knew. She had heard him once on the phone, begging Gloria Quilley not to end it, making promises he'd never keep… Hilary had guessed that much from the letters she'd found. But for all Hilary's resentment of her husband it was on to Gloria that her hatred and contempt had latched. If that was unfair, the unfairness was the price of their family remaining together. That, and this make-or-break summer on Uncle John's island. Here, without the props of ordinary life, the routines and camouflages gone, they would see what, if anything, remained. What was strong, what was weak. What was left of love in them.

Halfway up the steep hill out of the Haven, turning a corner, they came upon the white camper van. Slowly as he was driving, Geoff had to brake, then back the car downhill a little before creeping round on to the verge.

"Careful, Geoff, you're inches from that wall," warned Hilary, but Geoff was a master of the tight manoeuvre and crept a little closer just to show her. Beyond them, the young man was leaning into his van's bonnet.

Geoff stopped beside him. "Need a hand?"

The young man did not reply. He seemed not to have heard.

"The hill too much for her, was it?"

"Who?" the man responded this time, looking a little startled. "Oh, the camper? Yes, maybe. Don't worry, I've a good idea where the trouble lies."

"We're going up to the Robinson place. Hop in, if you want to phone for a mechanic – we'll give you a lift."

The man glanced at their car, in which every spare inch of seat space was taken up by bags and boxes.

"I don't think there is such a thing on Sweetholm," he answered tangentially. "A mechanic, I mean. Thanks, but I'll just roll it down off the road. I'm sure the farmer will give me a tow once he sees I'm blocking his gate. I can walk the rest of the way."

"You're not staying near John Robinson's place by any chance? If so we'll be neighbours."

But no, the man was not staying nearby. Geoff prodded him with further questions. Was this his first time on the island? Did he perhaps intend to camp, and where?

"I'll be with friends," he replied, with an abruptness he did not bother to disguise.

"You see, Geoff, in places like this even the tourists are sullen," remarked Hilary as they drove off.

"He wasn't sullen at all. Remarkably good-humoured, considering. Could have done with a shave, though."

"His clothes were falling off his back. And men like that travelling alone, well – you never know, do you?" Here she shot a glance at Tansy in the mirror. "You never know what they're like."

Tansy felt obliged to say, "He *wasn't* alone though, was he?"

"Pardon, Tansy?"

"He wasn't alone. He had a girl with him, didn't he? In the back."

"I didn't see anyone," replied her mother, as though that settled the matter.

"She didn't get out during the crossing," said Tansy. "But she was there just now. You must have noticed her."

It had been obvious enough, after all. The floral cushion cover pinned over the van's window had been lifted, and a small white face had shown there, peering curiously into a light that seemed too painfully bright for it. A beautiful child, of four or five. There was no doubt. But those eyes, so large and dark, had no lids with which to squint the light away, so that this girl could do nothing but stare and stare. A shocking, as well as a beautiful, face. But for all her staring, Tansy did not think the girl had seen them either.

Within two minutes they had reached Uncle John's smallholding. At first they missed it entirely, hidden as it was by a high stone wall and a hairpin entrance. But Tansy happened to look back and see what was only now visible, a sign with the words *Crusoe's Castle* painted in black calligraphic script.

"Oh, Geoff, it's *beautiful!*" said Hilary.

It was two storeys of the local limestone, a solid, yeomanly building declining into a sprawl of brick and mortar, a woodshed and a barn.

"Well, this *is* more like it," breathed Hilary. "The photos don't do it justice."

"And the inside's a gem," said Geoff. "Carved panels, hangings, all the rest of it. If anything, John's gone a bit overboard. Too fancy for round here. If it was up to me—"

"Yes?" prompted Hilary.

"Well, I'd strip it down a bit. Do something cheap and cheerful."

"Yes, you *would,*" said Hilary. "Cheap, especially."

If this shaft was aimed over Tansy's head, it missed. Gloria Quilley's Day-Glo taste in clothes had given Hilary a convenient handle for her scorn. Sighing, Tansy followed her parents up to the front door. With luck, the house would be startling enough to make them forget their tedious, half-unspoken row.

The heavy knocker brought no response. Geoff glanced to right and left, lest John might be crouching in the undergrowth. "Halloa!" he called. He stepped back from the door and began peering through the bullet-glass windows.

"Someone's got green fingers," said Hilary, admiring the window box. Looking at Tansy, she added, with a sudden breezy cheeriness, "Come on, Tansy, squeeze a smile out of that long face. This is meant to be a holiday."

Tansy saw that her mother was taking some pleasure in John's non-appearance and Geoff's discomfort. Another bad sign. But she smiled back.

"Mr Robinson, is it?" said a voice behind them.

Geoff turned, looking startled. Recovering himself slightly, he guessed at the name of the tall man before him. "Mr Jones?"

"Call me Davy," said the man, whose vast, tanned hand had already engulfed Geoff's slim white one and was shaking it with a heartiness that bordered on ferocity.

"Of course. John mentioned how helpful you've been to him."

Outdoor work had weathered Davy Jones's skin. His face was obscured by a long Viking beard that tapered to a point. Pale blue eyes smiled at them and lips, surprisingly full and childlike, grinned at Hilary and Tansy in turn as Geoff introduced them. "I'm sorry I wasn't here to meet you – I lost track of the time. John said you'd be here for twelve."

Davy produced a keyring from his pocket.

"What castle dungeon did you get *that* from?" Hilary asked with a gasp.

Davy looked apologetic. "John likes the drama of it, I think – the old cellar door, this is, with a lock to match."

"Isn't John in?"

"Didn't he tell you?" asked Davy Jones in surprise. "He left two days ago."

"He *what?*"

"They changed the date of his cruise at the last minute. It was panic stations here, I can tell you! Didn't he get in touch?"

"He did not!" groaned Geoff. "He was meant to be spending this week showing me the ropes. What am I going to do now?"

"I'm sure you'll get the hang of it," said Davy. "This was my uncle's house – I more or less grew up in it, so I know what goes where. Don't despair! We'll sort things out between us."

And very quickly he had found the massy key that opened the house, and he and Geoff were off on a tour of boilers, stopcocks and fuse boxes.

"Runes and druids," commented Hilary ironically as their heads sank below the trapdoor to the cellar. "Come on, Tansy, we have a house to explore."

"What about Uncle John? He can't just have gone off like this, can he?" Tansy had been expecting a full-scale argument over the blunder and this calm of her mother's was suspect.

"I hardly expected that any plan cooked up by John and your father would go smoothly. Look, here's the master bedroom."

Half an hour later Geoff returned, beaming. Tansy heard a door slam and the crunch of Davy Jones's feet on the gravel.

"See what I mean?" Geoff began. "So much for the islanders being stand-offish. Salt of the earth, that man! He's given me all kinds of help. Told me about feeding the Jacob's sheep and the hens, where the account books are, everything."

"Who is he exactly?" Tansy asked.

"Davy Jones? Calls himself the Nature Warden, but he's really the island's general handyman, I gather. None too bright, perhaps, but a heart of oak!"

"Then you've fallen on your feet again," said Hilary.

"*We've* fallen on our feet," Geoff pointed out.

Hilary shrugged. As Geoff pottered off, Tansy saw the set of her mother's face, momentarily bleak and distant. She said gently, "Are you sorry you came?"

"Sorry?" said Hilary. "No! Why do you ask?"

"It's just, you and Dad – you seem a bit... Well, you know how they said we had to break the cycle—"

"Not another word!" said Hilary, playfully putting her finger to Tansy's lips. "For myself, I intend to have a wonderful time. I advise you to do the same." And to Tansy's wonder Hilary flung herself on to the big double bed like a child. It was beyond understanding. But when Hilary laughed Tansy found herself laughing too, and burrowed under the covers to chase her mother's oh-so-ticklish feet. And they were giggling as they hadn't done in years, since the time before Gloria.

The sun was shining on the dust motes thrown up by the bed. The motes spiralled up out of the window and outside Tansy could hear the swooping gulls and their chatter, and she thought: I am going to remember this moment always. Because everything is so simple and so perfect.

That was when Tansy truly believed it. She realised that until then she had never thought they would escape from Bristol and from all that Bristol now meant. Even the thought of the place had a sour taste. Her best friend Kate had been compiling a list of secret names, spells to be cast on the unsuspecting. She half-believed she was a witch. But Kate had been making bad friends lately and it came into Tansy's head that she'd had a lucky escape.

A lucky escape. Yes, the phrase was a tempting one. Dad had escaped from Gloria and she had escaped from Kate. Lucky for them both.

"How do you like being marooned so far?" asked Hilary as she emerged, spluttering, from her cave of eiderdown.

"I love it," Tansy said.

3. The Asklepian

Who can say just when the warping of the world began? We are never free of miracles, of strange devotions, of cures that seem impossible. Our life is a nursery of wonder.

In the Caucasus an earthquake splits a mountain in two and reveals a hidden city carved from quartz. Its chairs and doorways are made for giants and the skeletons in the great sarcophagi, torqued and braceleted in gold, are more than seven feet long. An ancient man is discovered in an Appalachian valley, still in breeches and hose and talking, verily, in the speech of his fathers. On the high fells some say it is a lynx they have seen, lolloping through the bracken: some a leopard; others keep their counsel and will not venture beyond the town lights. All over the world sleeping powers begin to stir: old beliefs find willing minds to lodge in. Dabblers in magic are shocked to find their spells taking hold with a new and horrifying potency. Unheard-of diseases spring up, insidious and always deforming. As if in recompense, certain people discover gifts of healing in themselves: the Order of Asklepius is formed. But the Healers are few in number and their powers are not infallible. Even Dominic Fowey would admit as much.

Sitting in his converted ambulance, Dominic smiled. After

the car with its inquisitive driver and lifetime of luggage had disappeared over the hill's crest up to the moor, he had tried the ignition once again. The engine had cut in with insolent promptness. She's playing with me, he thought to himself.

He eased the van back on to the road. Slowly, he chuttered uphill till the gradient flattened out and he saw the island's one metalled road snaking westward to the Tor. On his right a drystone wall ran for some distance, beyond which he sensed the presence of buildings, farm machinery perhaps. And a distant roaring, not of the sea.

He had one picture of Sophie, taped to the inside of his sunshield. She was not with Calypso. That would have been dangerous for everyone, a hostage to fortune. He smiled again, this time at himself. How superstitious the last few years had made him! Or just careful, perhaps – hard to know.

Now the ambulance was on the open moor, thin soil with gorse and heather, and sheep gathered in the shelter of the outcrop rocks that broke like little waves over the copper earth. He had not expected the wind up here, but it came in sudden buffets, knocking his van to the edge of the roadside ditches. Not welcome, he thought. She doesn't want me here at all. Ah, but she's too young to understand.

Glancing in the mirror, he caught a glimpse of a young girl as she moved about the tiny kitchen behind him. A coffee jar was knocked mischievously to the floor and a pair of near-lidless eyes stared back in challenge. The road ahead curved slightly. When he looked again, the girl was gone.

Her appearance had not fooled Dominic. Calypso would be dreaming now. The apparition in the van behind him had been a projection from her sleeping mind, no more. Probably the girl was just protecting Sophie.

All the same, these were warnings. He was being told to stay away.

He passed one of the small farms. They were all the same: the makeshift repairs, a yard in which a dog barked incessantly, the tractor's harvest of rust. A last half-generation was sticking to the old ways here. Their children were off to the mainland: they couldn't get out quick enough. Dominic followed this dispiriting road to its end, to the Tor's foot, and his destination.

The Manor was different. The blessing of money was obvious in its weed-free walls and wrought-iron gate. Here the roadside ditch became nothing less than a dry moat, suggesting a past still more grandiose. On top of the barn (in which he spotted a brand-new four-by-four) a weathercock shone like burnished gold. A radio mast reared yet higher. This was the home of Gerard Winstanley, philanthropist and sometime tycoon. Dominic, who took little interest in such things, had nevertheless heard of him – even before events brought him to Sweetholm.

Ten years earlier, Winstanley had quit his very public life in disgust and withdrawn to the island, where he had declared himself reborn. By now the Manor had evolved into a retreat for social misfits, a commune, even a kind of cult – depending on one's choice of newspaper. Two summers ago, Sal Renshaw had arrived with her son Harper. A year later Sal's friend Sophie – Dominic's only sister – had brought her infant daughter there.

Dominic, with a quarantine authority from the Commander of his Order in his pocket, was wondering whether he would have to take them all away again.

★ ★ ★

Sal sat cross-legged on the bed, with the crocheted blanket pulled over her shoulders. The blanket hung down and gathered on the floor in a dark blue pool, in the middle of which Calypso lay half-submerged. Calypso was asleep, or seemed to be. Her eyes were closed, so far as those eyes could ever be said to close. Her chest moved a little with her breathing, but her fingers worked the blanket ceaselessly. Sal watched them sift the wool, stab and pluck and skein it. Sal too was drifting toward slumber.

Sophie and Calypso. Last summer had made them in love with Sweetholm. How fearless Calypso had been of the bees as they gathered honey! Winstanley had been intrigued by her even then. They lived in a golden cage of memories: the harvest of wild flowers; the mead they brewed in huge glass jars, wafting with heather and thyme; Harper's wood and weed drift from the beach. Calypso's fingers, usually clumsy, had yet proved so clever at tweaking out a thread to just the right thickness, then letting the spindle weight twist down. Although she could not hold the needles properly, she loved the Jacobs' wool, losing her hand in the thickness of the new fleece.

At that time she and Sophie were only meant to be visiting, but the visit lengthened and the days grew shorter, and when the summer ferry stopped its run they were still there, and going back to England had become somehow unthinkable.

It was summer again, but a fire still smoked in the great hearth. The slate tiles were warm as skin. More warmth fell from the lozenge of window light, into which Sal's feet just crept. A string of red glass beads threw a loop of light down, enchained the child's neck and waist. Harper would be back soon and Sophie was still talking outside. Her visitor said little, but his voice implored her, and Sal could hear his words over the scarlet embers' hiss.

"I haven't come to spy on you!"

"No one accused you, Dominic."

"Then why are you so suspicious?"

He was pacing about on the slabs, moving round Sophie, who would be sitting so still by now. Sal knew her well, how she would shrink back from a raised voice and make herself small and hard as a pebble. Sophie had a bit of that tough magic. And she wasn't frightened, even if he seemed to be laying some kind of doom on her.

"Come into the house, Dominic. Let's talk there."

He said in a new, hesitant voice, "But Calypso, she's asleep."

"It's all right. Come in."

And the door opened, and in came Sophie with her brother's hand in hers, and he seemed to have given up the idea of freaking Sophie out, at least for now. Sal nodded to him and got up to poke the fire. Calypso's grey eyes flickered. Sal could see that Dominic felt awkward with her in the room. Let him. *She* wasn't going anywhere.

"Hi, Sal," he said. "It's been a while."

"Hello, pet. Are you staying?"

He put his backpack on the big pine table. The weight of it was a kind of answer.

"You've got a good place here," he said. Sal saw him looking it over. Paternoster over the lintel, joss sticks, the glittering witch ball. "You've been weaving spells to keep the bad guys out."

"The sea is our moat," said Sophie, smiling. "The cliffs are our castle walls. And Sweetholm is just what it says."

"Calypso looks content."

"She is. She's very content. Sweetholm suits her."

"She's got a kind of… *sheen* to her. I never noticed from the photos. Oh, Sophie—"

"—Dominic!" said Sophie simultaneously. They both giggled, like children. There was something going on between them that Sal could only guess at.

Dominic looked at her. "And you've given her this shelter, Sal. You're a good friend."

"I try to be. But we're not alone here. Didn't Sophie explain?"

"Oh, I realise it's a colony. Where is everyone? Where's Harper?"

"Getting supplies from the Haven. You probably passed him."

Dominic hesitated. "I don't think I—"

"He's twice the height he was. You wouldn't recognise him."

"She's right, Dominic," exclaimed Sophie, "it's been far too long."

At once they were talking. Sal watched them for a while, protective of Sophie, careful of herself. Dominic was the only one who could shut Sal out. Sophie did not even realise she was doing it. They had too much past to be able to go beyond it, a complicated family situation that Sal had more or less given up trying to understand. But sooner or later they would have to reach Sweetholm, and today. Sal pulled the blanket round her shoulders, lay back on the narrow bed, and slept.

★ ★ ★

Calypso likes the sea air. It fills her eyes with light. It splays her webbed fingers and sends her clambering up the sandy grass, the last dune before the ocean. There she goes, the little selkie child.

The first time she dived into the water, she cut it like a blade. It fell back and she danced on it. Sal felt Sophie beside her, taut with the fear and the excitement, terrified that Calypso would turn her face out to the horizon. She might swim to that horizon and the air would flit with birds, and the porpoises would nuzzle her belly. She would glide on and forget herself, and her legs, with their duck-footed clumsiness, would melt into one, and she'd shiver in a dazzle of far water and be gone.

But it didn't happen that way. When Sophie could stand it no longer, she called Calypso back.

"Sing, Mummy, you have to sing to me!"

Dutifully, Sophie sang: she sang a song Davy Jones had taught her, about a fisherman who was starving. He was so weak that he did not have the strength to pull his fish into the boat and he had to persuade it to jump in of its own good will. And when the fish did that, its belly opened and out poured a mass of golden coins, and the boat almost sank under the weight of all that gold.

But Sophie's boat did not sink: Calypso allowed herself to be reeled in on that thread of song, though as soon as her feet touched the beach she fell, as if she could not bear her own sudden weight…

"I don't know what you're playing at, Sophie."

It was Dominic's voice: exasperated, chiding. Waking suddenly, Sal leapt in. "She's playing at being happy for the first time in her life. You should try it."

"Sal, please! I'm not here to make trouble. But on this island, of all places! To bring *her*, here!"

"What's wrong with it?"

"A few years ago you'd have died rather than be seen in a place like this. Some millionaire playing at gurus and all of you crying 'Shantih' at his feet."

"From you, this is rich!" hooted Sophie.

"But an island! After Joe, you should be going as far inland as possible."

Sophie grunted. "That would be running away."

"And Sweetholm is the thick of things?"

"It suits us. You think we don't deserve a break?"

"Of course you do." He came and sat beside her. "You can't guess the seventy ways I worry about you both, Sophie. And whatever you did, you'd get me turning up probably, trying to show you different."

Sal put her arms round Sophie. "Haven't you bullied her enough for now?"

"It's all right, Sal," said Sophie. She looked from one to the other and shook her head. "Let's show Dominic the house he has come to, at least."

When the footsteps had dwindled, Calypso sat herself up,

back against the stone pedestal. She pulled the crocheted blanket from her legs. She saw nothing that displeased her: a satin glimmer of reflected fire, a loop of scattered window light over the soft fur. Her toes stretched, her feet and legs stretched out together. She was glad to be alone and out of the dream-maze. Had that been... had it been... Uncle Dominic? Had it? And had she been with him in a hospital, a hospital on wheels that made her remember frightening things? Or had that been just a dream?

Calypso tucked her knees together and hooked her hands round about her shin. Other people, she had begun to learn, had dreams that stayed dreams. They were lucky, those people.

Her dreams always came true.

4. The Cursing Candle

The first things to stir at Crusoe's Castle next morning were Tansy's toes, which had broken free of the covers and found the air too cold. Tansy opened her eyes and saw them waving at her from the far end of the blanket. She had been put in one of the attic rooms, with a slanted ceiling and a dormer window.

She got up and tried out her view. From the open window she could hear the gulls wheeling, scavenging in the bins at the back of the house. One passed so close she could see the feathers of its outstretched wing, and the dribble of loose meat in its beak. No use even guessing what *that* had been when it was alive. Behind the gulls there were other sounds: the bleating of sheep from the field next door. And always, just too low to distinguish, a murmur of the sea. Even now it was spilling into the gulleys and on to beaches, scooping caves out of the rock not far away. On each side of this narrow island, from the north and south coasts it rose and arched over their heads, a dome of sea talk, of bee slumber, just out of sight.

There was much to do at the smallholding. Uncle John had left affairs in a disorderly state. Supplies of food and drink were low, the linen needed sorting and Hilary had declared the kitchen a war zone. And Davy Jones's showing Geoff the ropes seemed to involve spending most of their time in a shed at the bottom of the garden. Tansy lazily contemplated the possibility of escape.

In the yard the house's shadow lay flat and broken-backed where it rose against the angle of the barn opposite. To her right stood the spur of whitewashed brick where Uncle John had set to building guest rooms. Davy Jones had referred to this scoffingly as John's Folly. For there had been no guests.

"Nor ever will be, I reckon, not to speak of. If there's a guest here it'll be some rambler who forgot the time and missed the ferry back."

"But *why?* Look at this place – it's beautiful! They should be flocking here."

"Ah, well, you're seeing it at its best. But the weather…" Davy Jones mumbled something about the weather, but it was lost in his beard. "Once you get a reputation…"

This trick of mumbling dumbness was already familiar and Tansy knew better than to pursue him into its thickets.

One part of the reason had emerged later that evening, though not from the mouth of Davy Jones. They'd gone to the pub in the Haven. Two locals were playing dominoes in the public bar. Each sat with a half of stout that looked, as Geoff observed, more likely to evaporate than be drunk, at their rate. Once Hilary, using the excuse of an enquiry after toilets, had tried to prise open a conversation. The domino players had fallen silent and watched her, as one might watch a spider spinning.

Tansy did not merit even that much notice. Gazing at the lights on the fruit machine nearby, she had heard them mull over her Uncle John. "Not a patch on Owen Jones. Not a patch on Davy either. There hasn't been a decent crop raised on that land since Owen Jones fell ill."

The fruit machine said: *Welcome to the Pleasure Dome*, and cascading lights dazzled Tansy in the half-darkness. And the old men were peeling away the farm's history, through the Jones who kept it before Owen Jones, and the Jones before that who was crushed by one of his own pigs, back to ancient Hwyl Jones who built the place. And how it was a shame it had gone to mainlanders, and how things had never been right with it since.

Though it was early morning Davy Jones was already about, helping himself to bacon and eggs from the kitchen. Someone (Davy probably) had already mopped down the floor.

He saw the surprise on Tansy's face and laughed, a big Viking laugh. "Muzzle not the ox as it treads the grain," he said. "I've been helping to look after this place so long, it's become a habit." He sat down to eat in the big armchair in the living room.

"Haven't you a house of your own?" asked Tansy.

"Everything's under control," said Davy, a piece of fried bread pouched in his cheek. "The milking's done, and I have other people to help me. It's like that, Sweetholm. Everyone mucks in, like. You'll find out."

"It sounds a very friendly place." Tansy watched him pour himself more tea, four sugars. She decided she would try to find these friendly islanders – if their friendliness wasn't reserved for each other.

She entered the hall. Immediately opposite, her father's brother, Uncle John, looked down at her from a large framed photograph, in which he was being awarded a trophy of some kind. Since he was wearing a wetsuit, Tansy supposed it must be for diving, though it was hard for her to think of paunchy Uncle John as athletic. She straightened the frame, which had become lopsided, and this led her to examine all the frames on the wall.

One was a map of Sweetholm, dated 1904. A century of grubby fingers had worn the Haven away entirely, but on either side Tansy saw the paths wind down to the cliffs. Westward, the moor was scattered with smallholders' cottages, then the Tor, on either side of which the island petered out in dubious marshland, sound pebble beach that swirled into the hungry sand. The old priory church was marked 'Ruins'. A ten-minute walk south would take her to Palmerston's gun battery. The Haven lay ten minutes to the north.

Sweetholm had a past, of sorts: a past that exceeded its future. After the novelty of yesterday it was the island's grim smallness that struck her now. Three months. That was a long time, especially if there were to be arguments. Would Mum and Dad get on here? Would they? They had started so well, with such good intentions. But already there were signs, which Tansy knew too well to be able to block out. Geoff's defensiveness, the sarcasm that sometimes seemed as involuntary in her mother as a tic.

Back in Bristol there had been ways to escape the situation. The bus to the Mall, movies, friends' rooms where she could take refuge. Especially Kate's. Trouble was, Kate wasn't her friend any more – not since it came out about Geoff and Gloria.

Tansy couldn't blame her for that. After all, Gloria was Kate's mother. What was worse, Kate had known nothing, all that time. But she guessed how much Tansy had known.

"Why didn't you tell me?" Kate had demanded at last.

Kate hadn't spoken to her for days. Finally, Tansy had been allowed into Kate's room. Usually there was music playing, but today she could hardly speak for the silence.

"Why didn't you tell me?" Kate's voice was toneless, like the voice of a machine.

"It's just, I didn't want—"

"You *knew!* We were meant to be best friends. No secrets, remember?"

"Kate, I never wanted to hurt you."

"If you'd been in my house that night you'd have seen what hurting was. My Dad was sobbing, begging her to tell him it was all lies."

"I really thought they were going to end it. Then no one would have been hurt. Oh, Kate, I'm so sorry."

"Go on, Sellotape it with a 'sorry'. I bet that's just what your dad does too."

That had *really* hurt. But Kate didn't guess the whole truth even then. Tansy didn't tell her that the whole affair had been started by the Cursing Candle. And that was odd because the candle – all the magic, in fact – had been Kate's idea to begin with.

Kate Quilley had always been given to fads. At first her parents probably dismissed the incantations and the supernatural gewgaws that had suddenly appeared in her room. They would soon be gathering dust, they assured themselves, like the well-thumbed shelf of *Screams for Teens* that had preceded them. So they were not too anxious when Kate came home one day with a fat church candle, even though the cabalistic signs on its side were said to have been daubed with cockerel's blood. "She'll grow out of it," they sighed.

"It's a Cursing Candle," Kate explained to Tansy later. "One step up from wax dolls – and much more stylish. All you need to do is take a totem from your enemy and burn it. Then watch them droop and die."

Tansy sounded faintly shocked, as she knew Kate wished her to. "Have you tried it out?"

"Not yet. That's the trouble," Kate complained. "I can't think of anyone I hate enough."

"Except for Mr Podgery," said Tansy wearily as Kate's hamster began yet another workout on his wheel in the corner of the room.

Kate watched meditatively as the plump little rodent galloped and clanked.

"What a wicked mind you have," she said at last.

For years Kate had begged her mother for a pet. She had

dreamed of a pony of her own, a dog, perhaps a kitten. She settled for a hamster in the end, though by the time Gloria relented Kate had almost lost interest. Four years later, Mr Podgery's demands for food and clean bedding were more than she could bear. "If he was a human being he'd be over a hundred by now!" she would exclaim petulantly. "Roll up and see the world's first immortal hamster!"

So they began with Mr Podgery. Kate and Tansy took a clipping of Mr Podgery's hair and funnelled it into a twist of paper. The flame from Kate's candle burned green as they lit it, whispering words of power. Inside its little paper coffin the hair crackled. Mr Podgery was belting round his cage as though the very devil were at his heels.

"I don't like this, Kate. We shouldn't have done it."

"No one forced you." Kate's eyes were shining. Each reflected a small green lick of flame.

"I know. I feel sick. I know it's stupid."

"It's only a bit of fun," said Kate when it was over.

"I know."

Nevertheless, the next morning Mr Podgery was dead. His legs were sticking up like wishbones. They put him in a shoebox and buried him near the compost heap.

For a good while afterwards neither of them mentioned the Cursing Candle. They pretended nothing had happened and at first pretending was easy. There were plenty of other things to claim their attention and exams were coming up. It was six weeks later that Kate came home livid because of the school play, where Carol Sage's superior projection had robbed her of the chance to play Juliet opposite Frank Bonetti.

"You know Mr Finlay's always had a soft spot for Carol," Tansy consoled her.

"Never mind," said Kate. She was dangling Carol's choker from one finger. "Let's see how she does without her voice."

"You wouldn't!" said Tansy in alarm. She understood at once what that smile meant.

Kate was already arranging the candle in the middle of the table. "Watch me."

"Be serious, Kate! Mr Podgery – remember...'

"It's all right, I only want to give her a head cold."

"Mr Podgery got more than that."

But Kate had already made a new funnel of paper and now she was slipping the bead choker into it. She lit the candle and flicked the wax away from the writing on its side. Finally she held the paper funnel over the flame.

The choker would not easily burn and more than once Kate had to poke it down towards the candle with the end of a pencil. When it finally caught it was with a green-blue flame as the plastic melted and dripped into the wax. It smelt foul.

All the time Kate was urging infections to take root in Carol Sage's throat. "Come bronchitis, come halitosis!" Tansy tried to laugh – but Kate shot her an angry look. "This is serious, Tansy! Come tonsillitis, come you spirits of phlegm..."

It was a good spell. Kate was a natural: it was easy to see why she thought she deserved that part. In the following days, she and Tansy examined Carol closely for signs of encroaching fever. However, Carol and her voice remained unharmed. The play was played, Carol and Frank found true love, and walked around in dreamy smirking bliss. Kate fumed for a while, then forgot about Carol and the Candle too. She had moved on.

Tansy took up tapestry. She took up sketching. She discovered a talent for caricature and sold sketches to her friends. Planning a career for herself in Montmartre, she began to wear a floppy hat and occasionally a feather boa. Kate, by this time, was a mistress of the Tarot and in the evenings they had begun to collaborate on a special pack of their own. First, Tansy would draw a face, then on the reverse side Kate would inscribe her occult symbols. Friends, teachers and family would all be captured, and – although Kate and Tansy resolved to use their power exclusively for good – all would be brought under their sway. "It's an experiment," Kate would insist, "in sympathetic magic."

One evening in November, Tansy was working on a sketch of her father's face. They were in Kate's bedroom, which had become more Gothic than ever in recent months. Gloria had forbidden matt-black wallpaper, but had been unable to stem the invasion of horned skulls and astrological posters that had transformed the place into a witches' den. Thirteen candles flickered across the scene.

"What do you think?" said Tansy, pushing the card across the table. "Have I got him?"

"Not bad, my friend, not bad. The way his bottom lip hangs down! I hope it's not genetic."

When Kate left the room Tansy had taken Geoff's card back again. She paused. Something was wrong with it. Turning it over, she realised what. She had already used the reverse side the previous evening, to draw Gloria. Silly – she must have taken it from the wrong pile. Gloria didn't look much like Gloria any more, for that matter. The sketched face was darker than she'd thought, and rounder-mouthed. Kate had written under it: *La Papesse*. Briefly, she wondered whether to Tippex Gloria out. But she knew Kate would never stand for it. The hidden image would cause no end of psychic interference.

With a sigh, she held the card to the nearest candle until it sprang into green flame. It was a moment before Tansy recognised the crimson traces of a cabalistic symbol painted on the candle's side. She pulled the card out at once, with a yelp of fright. It was too late, of course. The card flapped and writhed in the flame's heat like a living thing. It curled over on itself, forcing her to drop it on the table. The last thing Tansy saw, before the card lost itself in ashes, was the pair of sketches she had made twining into each other – her own father and Kate's mother, their faces fracturing and merging in the heat.

The next day Tansy came upon Frank Bonetti wandering across the school field. He was on his own. His skin had the blotchy complexion of one who has been crying, hard. At the back of Tansy's mind there was already a note of alarm, a warning to stay silent and walk by. He watched her pass. A little further on, though, a girl from Tansy's class had noticed her and was waiting.

"What's up with him?" Tansy heard herself asking. She looked back at Frank Bonetti. "He been dumped or something?"

Gossip. Please let it be ordinary, who's-going-out-with-who gossip.

"You haven't heard?" said Tansy's friend. "Carol's in hospital." The concern in her voice couldn't disguise her eye-bright excitement as she told the story.

Carol and Frank had been fooling about with Frank's skateboard, on the footpath down to the park. It had been getting dark and Carol, squatting on the board as it ran downhill, hadn't seen the horizontal bar of the cycle barrier.

Tansy stood and listened.

"It got her in the throat, Tansy. Her windpipe!" Eye-Bright looked at her in awe. "They don't think she'll ever be able to talk again!"

5. The God-Botherers

"Why did you come *now*, Dominic? Why did it take you four years to start looking for me? Did you care if I was alive or dead?"

It had taken only one night to unravel Sophie and Dominic's truce. Calypso was still in bed – although her open window overlooked the lawn on which Dominic, Sophie and Sal sat, watching the foragers buzz about the hive.

Dominic glanced quickly at Sal. "I knew you were alive."

"Of course, you've got a direct line to God! So why didn't you know how *miserable* I was?"

"I knew that too," Dominic muttered.

"And you didn't think to drop me a line, to visit? To phone, even once?"

Dominic bit back a word. "Where I was there were no phones. And you didn't exactly leave a forwarding address. Life is not a game of hide and seek. While you were having your teenage rebellion, half the planet was crashing into ruin. You are my sister, Sophie, and I love you. But when I put your fate against the floods, the poison algae, the triple plagues—"

"You're dribbling, Dominic," said Sal.

"Put it in that scale and one person's misery just doesn't

register. You and I don't matter much to the world. No one person matters."

"Screw the world! I needed you more." Sophie threw the words at him like plates. Dominic let her. She would get tired, as she always did.

"At least," she said, "you came here eventually."

Dominic did not reply. He stroked the rim of his glass. Sophie heard the silence, and something unspoken in it. "Why *did* you come?" she asked.

"I sent for him," said Sal beside her.

Sophie stared at Sal. Her mouth dropped.

"She did the right thing, Sophie," Dominic began – but the look on his sister's face silenced him.

"I can't believe this," she said, with a moan of despair. "I thought I could trust you, Sal."

"It was Calypso," Sal began, "the things that were happening to her. I was scared. For her and for you, Sophie. I couldn't think of anyone else to ask. After that time with the music—"

"Music?" interrupted Dominic. "You didn't tell me about that."

Sal looked to Sophie for permission. Sophie held her gaze, then tossed it aside. "Tell him, then – tell him everything."

Sal turned to Dominic. "It was about six months ago. This place wasn't quite the same then. There were more passers-through, sneaking a holiday at Winstanley's expense. We didn't see so much of Winstanley himself. One was a nasty piece of work, a guy called Neil. We named him Masher. Just a joke at first, but later we found out he'd broken his parole and pulped a social worker's face. He was trying to lie low, but someone like that can't be anywhere without trying to take control. You never knew when he was going to take a swing at you. Most of the time he was drunk though, lying in his room with the speakers full up. All that beauty outside and he might as well have been in prison. The time Calypso was ill last Christmas, he kept everyone on edge with that machine-gun music. Sophie begged him to stop. He just pushed her out of his room, cracked her head against the stairs. Calypso saw that."

"Now," interrupted Sophie, "we don't know if Calypso had anything to do—"

"Next morning we found him lying in bed. The tape was going round and round in the machine, but no sound except the hum of the speakers turned up full. We played it again afterwards. There was no sound on that tape, only the spindle squeaking—"

"Gulls," said Sophie. "It was the gulls outside the window."

"There was a trickle of blood coming from Neil's ear. When we woke him he didn't seem to know who he was. He couldn't hear us at all. They said he had a perforated ear drum. As though a grenade had gone off just by his head, they said. Only none of us had heard a thing…"

"You can't think Calypso would do a thing like that deliberately," Sophie muttered.

"And something else. His arm was covered with little scratches and bite marks. A stoat, Davy Jones thought. But—"

"Don't tell me, there are no stoats on Sweetholm," Dominic said.

Sal grimaced. "Calypso has no guile. When Sophie asked her, she didn't try to hide it. She just said, 'But Mummy, he pushed you! He pushed you, Mummy!' Those big eyes staring. It broke my heart."

"What do you say, Sophie?" asked Dominic at last.

Sophie sighed. "I knew Calypso had done it – done it *somehow*. For me she'd taken on that bully and flushed him out. Oh, it frightened me. Somewhere in the pit of my stomach it sickened me. But… I was *proud* too. That power streaking from her!" She stopped and eyed him with dull hostility. "But you're the last person to understand."

Dominic looked puzzled.

"It's obvious, isn't it? My whole life I've been pushed around – by Mum and Dad, by teachers. And by you, Dominic—"

"Sophie!"

"Don't say you hadn't noticed! You were always so sure what you wanted. You always saw everything as your duty, God's will. How could I compete with that? I'm not blaming you – it was easier to fit in. I was just ordinary, you see? Nothing special about me, till Calypso came along."

"Till Joe swam into the rip tide," Sal corrected her.

Sophie spread her skirt about her, with the *fleur de lys*. "I guess." Her gaze lingered on Calypso. "And now that's turned sour too."

"Not if we can help it, Sophie."

"You see," Sophie said, suddenly urgent, "she doesn't understand at all. She's only a child. It's not her fault she's the way she is."

"I know that," soothed Dominic. "I came to help her, Sophie, if I can."

"I suppose once they would have called her a witch. We'd both have been for the bonfire in those days. Now, no one knows what to do with us. When she was born..."

"Yes? What is it, Sophie?"

Sophie tried again. "When she was born she was so small, with that coat of downy hair all over her scarlet body. The doctor kept giving her to me to hold, saying she would lose the hair in a few days, that it was nothing to worry about, it was commoner than you'd think, it was all right. He was scared I'd reject the little scrap, you see?"

"He didn't know Sophie," said Sal proudly.

"After Neil, Sal persuaded me to take Calypso back to the

mainland for tests, but it was still the same. They looked at her and all they saw was the fur on her legs, the eyes, the webbing of her toes and fingers. I overheard the nurses discussing her. 'How's the Beautiful Freak today?' they said."

"She hated hospital," said Sal. "They were talking about plastic surgery, grafts and all sorts. But when they lifted up her hand her fingers clenched so tight… It was pitiful, Dominic. She cried every time Sophie left the room. She wouldn't use words, just shrieked like an animal. And of course their instruments began to go haywire. That's when I *knew*."

"Knew what?"

"That we had to leave. They'd done all their tests, you see, dozens of them and they were trying to think of more. They didn't have a name for what she was and they couldn't stand it – not having a label for her. They were going to poke her about until she gave them a name. And I thought: this is an interrogation."

"And Calypso was a suspect, a criminal," said Sophie. "That's why I ran away…"

Between them they finished their confession. Dominic stared down the bridge of his nose into his glass.

"You suspect something yourselves, it seems," he said.

Sal hesitated. "You've been at Lasithi, in the camps. You've seen how the Red Leprosy strikes there. We've only heard rumours, the radio tells us nothing. But they say the children develop gifts sometimes. Prophecy, second sight. As if nature were trying to compensate them…"

"And you're wondering if that's true of Calypso?" Dominic shook his head. "Believe me, no. I've seen cases like that often. Those children! The eyes are cataracts, mother of pearl and weeping. But their magic is usually no more than a fakir's trick. They stick a red-hot needle through a limb where there is no feeling. They are cunning and pathetic, but their ambitions

43

stretch no further than the coin in your pocket. Calypso here is a different case entirely."

"Calypso is *not* a case."

"Sal, if you knew! I have to think that way, to keep sane. But Calypso—"

"Quiet!" cried Sophie. "I'm sure I heard her calling!"

Sure enough, Calypso had flung her shutters wide and was singing from the bedroom window above their heads:

"White bird featherless
Fell from paradise,
Over the garden wall..."

Her voice was a silken filament of sound, drifting in the air. It coiled invisibly about the garden, and silenced them.

"Here comes Lord Landless,
Takes it up handless,
Rides away horseless –
Off to the King's Great Hall!"

★ ★ ★

Dominic came in for breakfast, which in the Manor was taken around two long trestle tables, at no fixed hour. He sat near two young men who were helping themselves to cereal from an economy-size packet. He tried again to discover what kind of house he was staying in.

"Have you lived here long?" he asked them.

"Nine months," said one of the men.

"Nine months, one week and two days," added his friend. "To be precise."

"If you want precision."

"Otherwise, nine months will do."

Dominic smiled thinly. "Then you know Gerard Winstanley well?"

"It depends what you mean by knowing, doesn't it? 'What do I know?' – that's Winstanley's motto."

By now, half a dozen of the Manor's residents were staring at Dominic politely.

"You want to know about Gerard Winstanley?" asked the oldest, a woman of about forty.

"Haven't you seen him yet?"

"He lives upstairs with his computers. Playing the market."

"Surfing the net."

"Hacking into the World Bank," said another man, entering.

"Mike!" the woman reproved him. "You know he doesn't do that."

"No, no, I forgot," said Mike. "Winstanley's straight as a die."

"No one's forcing you to stay in his house."

Dominic made a tactical withdrawal into a slice of toast. As a matter of fact he had already gathered some information about the Manor's inhabitants, these and the rest of the hangers-on who used the Manor as a meeting place if not a home. Half a dozen tepees had been pitched in the meadow beyond the moat, in the shade of one of Sweetholm's few acres of woodland. Much of the time they appeared unoccupied, but occasionally he was able to spy the smoke from a camp fire and a furtive clustering of campers round it. A trip to the Manor's kitchen for water was not unheard of, nor was a trip for food, all of which Winstanley dispensed without question. The distinction between the campers and the Manor's more permanent residents appeared only nominal.

Of all the people who crossed the moat and walked the path to the Manor's front door only Davy Jones was a native of Sweetholm. The divisions between tourist and local, farmer and fisherman, meant nothing to him. The rest of the islanders stayed in their smallholdings, or the narrow strip of coastal buildings round the Haven. Dominic knew what they called the Manor folk. The God-Botherers – with a hint of a sneer in the voice.

By now, Gerard Winstanley had arrived at the breakfast table. He was a neat man in his fifties. Both chin and scalp were clean shaven and he was trimly dressed in close-fitting jersey and chinos. Dominic would have known him at once. His movements had an authority that immediately shifted the room's centre of gravity, though Winstanley was doing nothing more than stare ruefully at the bottom of a glass jar.

"Sometimes," he said, "I wonder why I put myself through it all. The blackcurrant jam's been scraped clean and I'm reduced to this pitiful shop-bought stuff." His prominent brow began to crease in lines of self-pity.

"It's because we make you feel young, darling. Admit it!" cried the older woman. On her way out she hugged Winstanley impulsively from behind.

"Old! You make me feel very old," said Winstanley and let a little milk spiral into his coffee. "These people treat me appallingly," he said, laughing, to Dominic. "You've no idea."

Dominic smiled.

"You bring that on yourself," said Mike. "All the dossers looking for an easy ride, the bigots down in the Haven, all that talk of the God-Botherers. You enjoy it."

"Let's say I'd go mad if I didn't have the stimulation you delightful people give me. I'd be a mad old fool hutched up with just a keyboard for company. But *enjoy?*"

He pulled a long-suffering expression. Dominic looked away, to the weathercock that pirouetted on the gable of the barn. The wind was turning the bird to and fro, sliding light off its gilded skin.

"I must fetch the rest of my things from my van," he said. "There's a storm coming."

"Harper will help you."

"I'd rather—" Dominic began, but seeing that Harper had already risen, added, "Thank you, I've very little to carry. But you're kind."

"Come to my office afterwards, Mr Fowey," called Winstanley as he left. "We'll need to talk."

Harper trotted after him into the yard, where the breeze was beginning to raise eddies of straw and loose paper. In fact, the back door of the van was hanging open too.

"Seems I've had visitors," Dominic remarked. Inside the van the floor and the basin were printed with crows' feet. A loaf had been hollowed out by their beaks and the food was tainted. Dominic looked behind him and saw Harper watching with grey eyes. He was, what – thirteen maybe? Sal had been right in her letter: an Aquarian child.

The state of the van seemed not to astonish Harper at all. Instead, he asked, "Is it true you came from Africa?"

Dominic started to strap up his sleeping bag, tightening a leather belt that had been skewered with an extra hole for the purpose. "Take this," he said, lobbing it down. He shouldered his small canvas bag. "Why? What do they say about me?"

"They say you've been working in the camps in Africa. You know – with the Red Leprosy. At least, that's what Sal told Mr Winstanley. She told him you were a priest."

Dominic smiled at that. "Crete, for the last year. Africa before. Why do you ask?"

"I'm interested. I thought maybe I should do that kind of work myself. I don't mean as a Healer. I want to be a nurse."

Dominic stepped down from the van and slammed the door shut behind him. "The Asklepians always need help. You've seen the TV I expect."

"There isn't a TV here. But when we were travelling, yes," Harper nodded. "Those big camps in the desert. Kids with

47

stumps where their hands and feet should be. They look so scared, always. I don't know how you carry on."

"How could we stop?" asked Dominic. He clasped his hands in front of him, staring at his fingers' ends. "The plague strikes at random – maybe one child in a family will fall, maybe a whole village. The army makes no exceptions: they're all trucked out to the isolation camp, to live or die. And most live, with our help." He sighed, as if that thought were melancholy. "The disease runs its course, they return home, they take to beggary. People give them food, although they hate them. It's bad luck to refuse and their curse is deadly. So they are kept just fed on the street corners. I don't know if I do them any favour in saving their lives."

"You do what you can," said Harper.

"What I was born to do, yes. Till now I've never doubted that my gift was a blessing from God."

Harper was working his way round to another question. Dominic could feel himself being weighed. Harper, he guessed, was not a boy who would trust anyone easily, for all his placidity. But his trust once bestowed might be tenacious. "What is it?"

"It's Calypso, isn't it? I mean, she's why you've come?"

"Calypso is part of the reason," said Dominic, choosing his words carefully. "Perhaps the main part – I'm not sure yet. There are other signs too. It's like any disease – the symptoms don't always seem to be connected at first."

"Disease?" For the first time Harper looked alarmed. "Just how ill is Calypso?"

"Calypso is not ill at all, not in the sense you mean," smiled Dominic. "But you see, we're standing in a place where the world's fabric has rubbed so thin…" He stopped, realising that Harper was not following his words. Perhaps he had said too much already.

"Soon," he said. "Soon we'll talk." Glancing at an upper window he saw Winstanley watching them. "Meanwhile, I think I'm expected."

6. Genesis

Davy Jones, that man of many parts, was in his workshop. The rooms he rented down in the Haven were small and cheap, and suited him grandly. Their shelves were crammed with buckets of glaze, picture frames, hammers, glue, brushes. Beach jetsam, too, in its various forms. Dawn would usually find him searching Sweetholm for shells and stones. He prized the glass from thick green bottles, treasured human hair. A row of plastic dustbins held five different kinds of clay. His kiln and potter's wheel were housed in one corner, though Davy Jones was a modeller rather than a thrower of pots. Carpentry was his true talent, in fact, and wood his truest love. Carpentry tools hung from hooks beside him now and he was using a fine chisel and mallet to block out a long, long nose in an old, old face. The grain of the wood helped suggest its age, an effect he would later enhance by skilful sanding and the application of certain oils. The face's skin, apparently wrinkled, would actually be as smooth as glass and as cold to the touch.

Though the weather was hot, Davy kept the window shut, for the work was private. The louvre blinds were shut also, so that a cream-beige glow was cast on everything within. If, indeed, anyone had managed to circumvent the window latch and make their way inside, they would probably have found Davy Jones easy to surprise, so engrossed was he in his work. But they would have received a sharp and surprising rebuke from the man with the chisel. This, more than anything he had ever done, was sacred work. In performing it, he was linking himself to something holy, something beyond himself. None of his acquaintance would have guessed it, but Davy Jones was earning admittance to a very select company: the company of masons, stone-haulers, beaters of airy gold, builders of high places. That was why his hands tingled with excitement, why the very water in his glass shone like nectar in the milk-white light.

He stood back from his workbench and breathed out softly, full of awe.

Davy Jones was making the face of a saint.

7. Winstanley Explains Himself

Gerard Winstanley's office, reached by a wrought-iron spiral staircase, occupied half the top floor of the Manor. The other half was his private quarters. When Dominic found him, Winstanley was standing at the stained-glass oriole window with his back to him. A large pine desk took up most of one wall. It was empty except for Winstanley's computer and fax machine, a few sheets of scribble and a paperweight in the shape of the god Ganesh. Other deities lined the walls: a variety of hunts, feasts, wars and seductions had been woven into tapestries and framed. In the corner above Dominic's head was a closed-circuit television screen. It was divided into six sections, each corresponding to a view of the Manor and its surroundings. It seemed that no one could approach the place without Winstanley's notice – or leave it.

Winstanley turned when he heard Dominic's tread, though he must already have been aware of him. "Your belongings are safely stowed?"

Dominic nodded. "Thank you."

"Safely gathered in before the storm." Winstanley glanced at the sky. "Though the storm, I think, has spared us on this occasion."

Dominic did not wish to discuss the weather. He remained standing.

"Well, we are honoured to have an Asklepian on the island. We all admire the work you people do. Your business here – it is of an official nature?"

"No, not official," said Dominic.

"You won't be putting Sweetholm in quarantine then?" smiled Winstanley – a little nervously, Dominic thought.

"Why would I? None of the proscribed illnesses is present."

Something in the way Dominic said it made Winstanley hesitate. "By which you mean that other illnesses are?" he suggested at last.

"That's not for me to say, Mr Winstanley. I'm a stranger here."

"You haven't come on a purely family visit at any rate," Winstanley persisted.

"I came because I was asked," said Dominic. "My sister needs me."

"Ah yes, well you're protective of your sister. That's very natural." Winstanley nodded sagely. "But Sophie is happy here, is she not? Has she said otherwise?"

"No. But Sophie isn't always the best judge of her own interests."

"There we must differ. But I can guess what you're driving at. A community like ours… I don't know what they say in the Haven but I'm sure there are rumours. The nights are long. Everyone likes a good story to while the time away."

"I haven't heard any stories and I haven't been to the Haven. What would they tell me?"

"Nothing very original, I imagine. That this is a brainwashing cult, that we're devil-worshippers, or waiting for aliens to land on the Tor and fly us to Andromeda," said Winstanley wearily. "Take your pick."

"None of which is true, of course?"

"My dear boy, does your sister strike you as brainwashed?"

"No," said Dominic. "No, that's not the word."

Gerard Winstanley sighed. It was not the first time he had had to explain himself. In fact, as he liked to point out, explaining oneself – really *explaining* oneself – was the first, last and most intricate of tasks. A lifetime's work! But Dominic Fowey's suspicion of him threatened to make this a tiring interview. He sat behind his desk with his fingertips just touching, his egg-shaped chin balanced delicately.

For his part Dominic too had been wrongfooted. The newspapers had given him quite the wrong expectations of Gerard Winstanley. The courtly and slightly old-fashioned figure before him was a surprise.

"As for money," Winstanley was saying, "don't imagine that anyone here has signed over their life savings to *me*. I have enough already and I've no wish to set myself up as a tinpot messiah. The fact is, I support all the people here. I'm using the proceeds of capitalism to finance an alternative life for the people who need it. For a month or two, a year, five – however long."

"So they're a kind of *hobby?*"

Winstanley smiled. "The whole point of this is to treat people with respect. Respect is everyone's due. You can't make a hobby out of people."

He sat back in his chair and made a sweeping gesture.

"Once this would have been called a religious retreat. Only now there's no religion, is there? Just the scraps that everyone fights over and calls by different names. As for the retreat part – well, I think of it as a facing up to, not a running away. The people here aren't cowards, they've had the courage to look for something more than the spoon-fed life. A lot of them have given up good jobs, as the world calculates these matters. Yes, they have problems to solve – but they've made the first step. I admire them, I really do. Every day I learn."

"And what have you learned about Calypso?"

Winstanley looked suddenly grim. "That she has had an evil time. That since she came to Sweetholm she has flourished. That everyone here loves her and will let no harm come to her. Aren't these the important things?"

"These answers do you credit, I'm sure," said Dominic, before adding suddenly, "Tell me, Mr Winstanley. You are rich enough ten times over to keep this place running. Yet I saw your name mentioned only weeks ago in connection with the Cronos take-over. I thought you had renounced that part of your life."

The question seemed to nettle Winstanley. "Even I am not a bottomless pit, Mr Fowey." He turned to the window overlooking the yard as though he were chewing over a point in his own mind. A seagull landed on the sill opposite. When Winstanley spoke again he was suddenly brisk. "Do you intend to stay here long?"

The seagull pecked at the white paint of the sill, then hopped.

"Do you, in fact, intend to stay at all?" Winstanley repeated.

"Do you object, Mr Winstanley?"

"Not in the least. We have the room."

"Thank you, but perhaps I'd better sleep under my own roof after all."

Winstanley shrugged. His attention had been caught by something down in the yard. Dominic followed his gaze. There was nothing to be seen except for his own white van. Only – only there was a small disturbance in the light around the van's bonnet. Then he too noticed what had drawn Winstanley. It was a smell, acrid and noxious – the smell of burning oil and rubber.

Winstanley turned to him. "I'm afraid, Mr Fowey, that your vehicle appears to be on fire."

8. Harper

Tansy followed the road away from the Haven. Her own long shadow preceded her. She did not know why she had turned in this direction when she left the house. Her first thought had been to descend the half-mile to the shops, to pick out a postcard maybe. Maybe write to Kate. But the westward road had turned her. Perhaps it was the idea of reaching the lump-headed Tor at the far end of the island. Though she knew it was really two miles away, it looked closer in this light, across this unflinching land.

Before she arrived, Tansy had expected to find in Sweetholm a wilderness almost untouched. Even now, she could imagine herself looking down from the Tor and seeing it as it had emerged from the swirling waters, the topmost slope of a drowned forest. The sea was still brown with the mud from those ancient roots. The river swept mud into the estuary, the tide imprisoned it and made it a thick, blind pool, now as then. A living had been scraped – how long, who knew? – from between the outcrop rocks. The island's plants were scavengers: cow parsley, alexanders, bindweed, ground elder. On occasion, the earth was harrowed by an ice wind from the north; more often the westerly rain bogged it and sent the precious soil in rivulets and sudden streams to the sea.

A scramble path cut under her feet, away down to the shingle. Cairns of droppings showed where the sheep had preceded her. She could even see one on the shoreline now. It was tugging at a long strip of green-dark weed. As Tansy neared the level of the beach the path turned and revealed a small bay. Boulders lay high as her head and round like slingshot. From there you could see out to the horizon and the bar that halved the sea before it, the white foaming line of lethal shallows.

The tide was out. When Tansy reached the bay she found the ground wet and the giant rocks were pimpled with limpet shells, shadowing pools of crab and weed. Further along, the shingle was strewn with the sea's jetsam, up to the weed-lined tidemark. One of the shadows suddenly raised itself upright and turned towards her.

It was a boy. He was her own age, or rather a little younger. A slight child, with blond hair that wisped up in the breeze as the hood of his thin coat fell back. He had been crouched beside one of the boulders, still as a boulder himself. Now he saw her too and grinned.

He came towards her, dragging a rope bag after. There were some bits of wood in it and something slimy that trailed unpleasantly through the grooved sand.

"I'm Harper," he announced.

There was something strange about the way he said it. It was as if he expected Tansy to recognise the name: as if everyone would know it as a matter of course. That was the effect of living on a small island, perhaps. More though, she felt he was making her welcome to a place that was his own – and that his greeting was the courtesy due of a host.

She nodded. "Tansy. What's in your bag?"

"A few bits of scavenge. Shells and stuff. You from John Robinson's place then?"

"How'd you know?"

"I'm a lucky guesser. I saw you arriving on the ferry yesterday." In answer to Tansy's look of puzzlement he added, "A couple and a girl. Davy Jones said you'd be along." He shrugged. "I was sort of looking out for you."

"Who did you say you were?"

"Harper... You'd better move up the beach, unless you want to get your feet wet."

The sea was sifting the rock pools. Tansy had not noticed its approach.

Harper said, "The ground's flat just here, the tide goes miles out. People think they're safe. They go out on the causeway, collecting shells. But when it comes back, the sea can outrun you. Been caught that way myself, almost."

"You live in the village?"

He shook his head. "To the west. Just at the foot of the Tor. Don't worry, you'll soon get used to the place."

"So they tell me." Tansy thought of the map in the lobby and how small the island had seemed there, like a spadeful of earth spilt by some careless giant intent on burying Britain. "Is there much to do here? I mean, places to see?"

Harper smiled. "This is a place, isn't it? Everywhere you go, you're in a place. All places are really the same." He added, "Change yourself instead."

This last phrase struck Tansy as a quotation – perhaps one that Harper expected her to recognise.

"You always lived here?" she asked.

Harper was crawling over the boulders by the cliff to get to the next section of the beach.

"Got to move or I'll miss things."

"You often come beachcombing?" puffed Tansy, as she landed beside him. Harper was at least a couple of years younger than her, she guessed. Back in Bristol he'd have been taken up with football and fancy trainers, and she'd have stepped past him with disdain. But in Sweetholm she could not afford to be choosy. Holidays changed things like that. Harper was company. He could show her things and looked happy to do it. She wished he would stay still, though. "Is this a hobby of yours?"

"Not a hobby, a job," said Harper simply.

"Someone pays you? For that?" Tansy looked sceptically at the contents of Harper's string bag, which were nothing more than some pieces of driftwood, shells and stones. Pretty, but worthless. Harper was in a world of his own.

"Davy Jones. You've met him," explained Harper.

"What would he want with that stuff?"

"He makes things – didn't you know? He's got a shop down by the ferry. Easter to October."

Tansy hadn't known that about Davy Jones.

"He finds bits of driftwood, shells, anything," Harper continued. "Stains the wood turquoise or blue and makes a bathroom cabinet, maybe, or a stool. Whatever the wood wants to be, he says. The wood's got its own plans."

"I see," Tansy said doubtfully.

"Sometimes he decorates it with dried weed, or string. Sometimes, say it's a mirror, he'll paint a mermaid on it. Easter to October people pay good money for driftwood. Something from the sea, Davy says, to take back to town and dust. If they pay over the odds it's up to them. They could have a stick of rock at half the price."

They had come to a steep rock, slimy with weed. Harper, familiar with its contours, climbed it as easily as a flight of steps. From the top he looked down at Tansy.

"You need a hand getting up here?" he asked, daring her to need it.

"I'm just fine."

"Suit yourself."

Tansy climbed the rock. In Bristol she belonged to a climbing club and spent each Tuesday evening scaling an artificial rockface in a disused church. Harper was gratifyingly impressed by her technique, she saw. On the next section of the bay he continued scouting the sand. For a few minutes Tansy watched him. Then something caught her attention. She called to Harper.

"What is it?" he asked.

"For your collection."

A spur of dark wood stuck out from between two stones. Sand-hoppers jumped on the yellow ground.

Harper was on his knees at once, scratching out the sand, and in less than a minute they saw it. What they had found was a tree branch. But the wood seemed almost to have been shaped. The first spur was one of five, a pointing finger.

"It's an arm!" shouted Harper. He dug enthusiastically.

Tansy did nothing. For the last minute she had sat staring, palms back on the sand. After her first touch she had recoiled.

"It was *soft!*" she said at last.

Harper had reached the elbow now. The wooden limb was in full view and really just a tree branch after all. Nothing that would have deceived a child. A crude resemblance to a hand. But it had deceived Tansy.

"It touched me," she breathed. "It was warm!"

With an effort Harper pulled the thing free of the sand and fell back with the branch on top of him. It was broken just above the elbow. If there had been a body to match, it would have been that of a giant, seven feet or more. A giant with brown, chiselled skin. What face would such a creature have?

Tansy did not want to think about its face.

Harper had agreed to meet Davy Jones at the Manor. Tansy followed him as he walked the cliff path to the moor, with the net bag slung over his shoulder. Tansy said little, that last mile. She found herself examining the ridges and cavities of the Tor, which gleamed before them now like an old, cold sun, pulling them in. How could anyone bear to live in its shadow?

They entered a concrete yard. The Manor buildings were ranged about them: the ancient house itself, barn, greenhouses, and the glimpse of a vegetable garden beyond. But Tansy did not have time to take this in, for at once the smell hit them. Fire! A camper van – *the* camper van from the ferry – stood in flames in the centre of the yard.

"Hell!" shouted Harper. He dropped the bag and ran to the wash-house. Tansy followed, not understanding quite what was happening. Harper shouted back breathlessly. The grass on Sweetholm was tinder. No fire brigade, either. If the whole island went up!

"The hose reel!"

Other people were beginning to emerge from the house. A hose was lugged out from the long greenhouses, but the man carrying it seemed not to know how to release the sprinkler. While he fumbled, a window of the ambulance exploded. More flames shot up and a sweet smell of plastic drifted out into the yard. A crowd was gathering: a woman with dyed red hair was trying to organise a human chain. People stopped running, submitted themselves to the task.

Only one person was not helping. A young man stood with his hands on his hips, watching the inferno from under the Manor's stone lintel. Tansy recognised him from the ferry and wondered why he stood calmly watching the destruction of his own vehicle. There was even a smile on his lips.

There was another face she recognised too. On the opposite side of the yard, just inside an open barn door. It was the little girl with lidless eyes.

The fire was out surprisingly soon. Tansy had been expecting an explosion of the kind she had often seen on television, with all the bystanders blown off their feet as the petrol tank went up, and bits of metal shooting out like party streamers. But the petrol tank survived. Only the driver's seat, the dashboard and the steering wheel had disappeared. Melted, virtually to nothing. A skeleton of springs and puckered plastic.

"That's going nowhere in a hurry," said one of the men.

"Looks like you're staying with us after all, Dominic," said the woman with the dyed hair. "You can't kip out in that."

The others gathered round, echoing murmurs of sympathy and invitation. "Yes, stay Dominic. We've got room."

"*No!* I wanted him to go away!"

The little girl from across the yard, silent until now, had erupted into a wail of frustration and despair. "It was meant to frighten him away!"

"Calypso – go back inside!" said one of the women sharply, with a quick glance at Tansy. "Sal, did you know she was awake?"

"You can't hide her all her life, Sophie," said the red-haired woman. "I'll try and calm her down."

"Dominic, I'm sorry," Sophie began.

"Sal's right," replied the man called Dominic. "You can't rein her in for ever. You must have known that." He contemplated the van, now dripping dry in a pool of water in the yard. "She very nearly fried me in there."

"She didn't mean to hurt—"

"I realise she's no idea what she's doing," interrupted Dominic. "That just makes her more dangerous."

He turned, and seemed to notice Tansy and Harper for the first time. "We'll talk later. I want to salvage what I can from this lot."

At that moment a figure detached itself from the huddle of firefighters and strolled towards Tansy and Harper. "Harper, what have you brought me?" It was Davy Jones. He glanced at the wreck of the camper van as he passed, but it evidently held little interest for him. Instead, he squatted beside the intriguing net bag Harper had been bumping along the ground. The arm-shaped branch had almost worked itself loose, fingering a hole in the netting. It pointed back at Davy Jones.

"Who have we here, Harper? A damsel, is it? A damsel in distress?"

"It'll cost you," said Harper.

Davy Jones tutted. "Tansy, have you teamed up with this one? He'll lead you astray." He was untangling the wooden arm from the loops of the bag and soon he held it out sunward, where it shed its loose sleeve of black weed. Tansy saw the gleam of the sun texture its skin. It was smooth and, if she dared to reach her arm out, still soft perhaps, to the touch.

Davy Jones stared at it, with an intensity that looked like desire. "And where exactly did you come across it? It's not your average beach drift."

"One of my spots," said Harper stolidly.

"Playing dumb?" Davy Jones ran the tip of his finger over the stiff, wooden palm. "And you're sure there was nothing else? Nothing like this lying about?"

"Like I said – it'll cost."

Davy Jones harrumphed. "This is oak. Last hundreds of years, this will, even in sea water." A fog of thought hung about him. But at last he looked up. "Yes, I'll pay you to show me where you found it. You and Tansy, eh? There may be more where this came from."

Tansy was staring at the little girl, tear-faced, who had shuffled out towards them. A shapeless cloak, or poncho, had been draped over her, and a wide-brimmed hat. She looked as if she had been playing at dressing up, but there was none of the swagger of make-believe in her progress through the yard.

"Harper, who is that?"

"That's your mascot, isn't it, Harper?" said Davy Jones.

"Her name's Calypso," said Harper.

The one they called Dominic stepped through the puddles of hose-water and picked up Calypso, so that her hat brim flopped over his head. "Come now, you're not angry with me, are you?"

Calypso pulled a face and writhed. "Put me down! Mummy! Sal! Put me down!"

But Dominic just laughed, even when she kicked him, her bare feet drumming on his midriff. "Careful! Don't you want to see the present I've brought you?"

The force of the kicks lessened slightly as Calypso took this in. "A present, Uncle Dominic? What is it?"

"You promise not to hurt me any more?"

"You made Mummy cry!" said Calypso, aiming one last blow to Dominic's ribs. But this was a mere gesture. "What have you got me?"

He pulled from his pocket a small box. Calypso squealed with anticipation, but Dominic said, "You can open it in the house. It's lucky I took it out of the van earlier, isn't it? You'd have burned it up."

"I'm sorry, Uncle Dominic." She threw her arms around his neck and kissed him. "I'll get you a new van. I'm saving up!"

Dominic laughed. "You won't find another like it, love. Not on Sweetholm. But didn't it make a good bonfire?"

"A lovely fire, Uncle Dominic. Look at all the rooks! They liked it too."

A dozen smut-black birds were circling, punched out on a fist of wind and tossed high. Their chatter out-hummed the generator in the barn.

Tansy found herself straining to catch a clear view of Calypso's face, but the wide brim of her hat shadowed it, except for the one moment when she looked up at the sky: and then it was laughing, her mouth pearled with perfect child's teeth. But her eyes were round as limpet shells and could not blink. Tansy turned to the other people, the five or six onlookers who stood like herself. Some were pierced with hoops of metal: in ear, lip, nose, eyebrow, navel, tongue. She felt suddenly nervous of this place, these people cloistered here beneath the Tor of Sweetholm.

Harper was tugging her sleeve. "You coming in?"

She glanced at the sky and saw how high the sun already was. "I should go back to the house," she said.

"Come and see Hermione first."

Hermione was a goat, Harper's favourite among the flock who provided the Manor with milk and cheese. She had short white hair and little stubs of horn shot from her tufted face. At the edge of the enclosure Tansy leaned forward, a wrenched fistful of grass in her hand.

"Hermione? Come here, Hermione."

The goat nibbled at her sleeve, green eyes demented. Harper flicked at its back with a stick. "Crazy thing. They'd chew up the whole island."

"Harper, what was wrong with that girl?"

Harper pretended not to understand. Then, in his own time, he let the penny drop. "They can't make up their minds about it. Nothing's wrong in fact. She's Calypso – that's her secret. Not like you and me, Tansy. Thank your stars you're ordinary."

"Did she really set that van on fire?"

"I expect so."

"How? Wasn't she indoors?"

"I expect she *was* indoors. That wouldn't stop Calypso. That's why we tread so wary round her tiny magic feet. 'Cos of the dances they can do. When Calypso dances, things move."

★ ★ ★

Calypso looked up at her uncle defiantly. "Where's my present?" she demanded. Her face challenged him to be angry.

64

Through the window behind her, Dominic could see the remains of his van. It was hard to believe the fire had taken place just twenty minutes ago: already the vehicle seemed rooted in the yard. It had carried him round half the world and would never move again.

He opened the box and drew out a silver bird on a chain. "It's a heron," he explained, as Calypso fingered it carefully. She said nothing at first. Then she looked up and smiled.

"Thank you, Uncle Dominic. Shall I wear it round my neck?"

"That's why I bought it. Where this comes from, they say a heron brings protection."

She came forward and kissed him. For a moment he saw her eyes from close up: the prismatic depth of them: golden, dizzying. "I still hate you for making Mummy upset," she said. "Thank you for the necklace."

She had slipped away, like water through his fingers.

"I saw – did you know? As I drove here, I saw you in the back of the van."

Calypso nodded cautiously. "I dreamed myself there. I saw you too."

"Do you always travel in your dreams?"

Calypso nodded again. "It's not so clear as that, not usually. And sometimes I go the other way."

Dominic hesitated. "The other way? What way is that?"

Calypso walked her fingers over the table, backwards and forwards. "I move sideways and slideways, Uncle Dominic. That's how I know what's going to happen."

"You see the future?"

"I see round corners sometimes. But I don't like it."

"No, darling?" asked Sophie. "What don't you like?"

"It's not nice," Calypso muttered at length, edging closer to her mother.

"What's not nice? Try to tell us," said Dominic as Calypso looked away.

"Enough, Dominic. She doesn't want to talk now."

"Have you seen something that frightens you, Calypso?"

"I'm not frightened!" Calypso retorted with scorn. "*She* doesn't frighten me!"

Dominic shot his sister a sharp look. "Who do you mean, Calypso?"

"The one who took Daddy! I've seen *her*, of course I have." Then she added, "Didn't you know she was on the island?"

"What's her name? Perhaps I should talk to her."

"She's not even real," Calypso scoffed. "Not yet." She paused, as if a thought were taking shape in her mind. "But she'd like to be."

Dominic took Calypso's hand and whispered, "Does she have a name – yet?"

"Stop it, Dominic! Can't you see she's talking about some made-up friend?"

Calypso had in any case lost interest. She made her heron loop the loop on its chain. Looking at her mother she smiled, squawked like a gull. "Look Mummy!"

"It's lovely, darling. You go and help Sal now. Uncle Dominic and I have to talk."

Calypso got to her feet and went to the door. But as she was leaning on it she turned to Dominic. And she asked, as she might have asked the name of a flower on the garden wall, "Uncle Dominic?"

"Yes, Calypso?"

"Do you remember wishing… I mean – do you think you'll ever try to kill me?"

★ ★ ★

At home, the Robinsons' island idyll had suffered a setback.

"The Jacobs have escaped, Tansy!" called Hilary as she saw her approaching. "Oh, where have you been? That foolish man, your father, forgot all the country lore he supposedly had bred into him and left the gate unbolted."

"Actually, I did bolt it," replied Geoff as he checked the fencing. "How those blasted sheep got out I've no idea. But they're back now, all accounted for and no harm done." Geoff uttered this rapidly and low, and clearly not for the first time. He straightened his back and rubbed at a patch of dry red skin that had recently flared on his forearm. "Have you been exploring then, Tansy?" He seemed glad of a chance to change the subject.

"Kind of…"

"Find any smugglers' caves? Sweetholm used to have its share."

"Not caves. I found a boy, though – Harper. Davy Jones knows him. He lives in a big house near the Tor."

"One of that lot from the commune, was he?" said Hilary. "I heard about them this morning. Down in the Haven Post Office they had plenty to say on that score."

"I can imagine," said Geoff, "broad-minded lot as they are. Mind you, I suppose they only see them when they go to collect their giros."

"What *do* they say in the Haven?" asked Tansy.

"It's more of a religious community, according to Davy," Geoff continued. "Harmless, he says."

Hilary pulled a face. "If it's on Sweetholm, Geoff will hear nothing against it," she explained to Tansy.

"You're right," Geoff laughed. "This is the kind of place I dreamed of living when I was a boy. Sea air, the cry of the gulls… I'd probably have spent my whole time looking for a treasure map."

Tansy looked at him pityingly.

Geoff noticed her expression. "This was a very piratical part of the country, for your information. Sweetholm has more history than you'd think."

"I'm sure it does."

"It's been a fishing port, a royal warren, a gun battery – there was even a priory, back in medieval times. Some rich knight set up a group of monks to come here and pray for his soul. They'd been going a hundred years when the Black Death wiped them out." Geoff stopped, to find that Tansy and Hilary were no longer paying attention. "I suppose God got tired of listening."

The phone was ringing in the house. Hilary went to answer it. "Hello?" they heard her say. "Is anyone there? Speak if you're going to!"

A moment later she returned. "Another silent call," she muttered.

"There've been others?" Tansy asked.

Hilary looked at Geoff. "Ask your father," she said shortly and walked back into the house.

"The second this morning," said Geoff. He too seemed suddenly tight-lipped. "I'm going to get the company to check the line."

The silence that followed was too long. Tansy had to break it.

"Dad?"

"Yes?"

"Things are all right, aren't they? With you and Mum, I mean?"

"Yes, yes, of course," replied Geoff, still half distracted.

"Only she seems – I don't know. Tense, somehow."

"It's the culture shock, Tansy. We always knew it would take time to settle after Bristol. It's hard to slow everything down to island pace. Your mind races. And sometimes you see things that just aren't there," he added significantly.

68

"So those phone calls—"

"—are a fault on the line. You'll have to trust me on this one, love." He grimaced and scratched at his arm. "Even if I don't deserve it."

"You do deserve it. I love you both, Dad."

Geoff hugged her. "And we both love you. You know that, don't you? Good."

But do you still love each other? thought Tansy sadly as Geoff went back to the Jacobs.

In the yard, half a dozen chickens were gleaning the cracks in the concrete, on the scrounge for seeds or insects. The hemlock beneath the wall nodded under the bees' feet. It seemed to Tansy that being here on Sweetholm was like living in a bubble: reflecting everything, not anchored to the world. Fragile, and so temporary.

"And it's my fault," she said savagely, under her breath. "All my fault."

Carol Sage was recovering well, they said. To look at her, you would hardly believe she had had an accident. She could smile and swallow solid food. She could make herself understood, was cared for and well loved. Her progress was remarkable.

But no – her voice was gone for ever.

Kate had wavered after the accident. For a month she had abstained from magic altogether. During that month another Polynesian atoll had been lost to the sea. Locusts had swarmed in southern Spain. Uncle John had entered a magazine competition for the first time in his life, and won a cruise to the eastern Mediterranean. Despite the changes that were creeping up on the world, ordinary life still functioned and its ordinariness was comforting. The buses ran, the shops twinkled at Christmas, the schools plied the same trade in physics and geography. Beyond the school gates, however, Tansy knew that both subjects had suffered a subtle transformation.

One day, Tansy had walked into Kate's room and found her scrying with a hollow stone and some horse brasses.

"The future's none too bright," said Kate. Her eyes were black. Panda eyes.

How ridiculous she looks, thought Tansy. She picked up a plaster skull and shook it. It rattled a little.

"Was it us?" she asked. "Did we do that to Carol?"

The panda eyes blinked. "Coincidences happen. This one took two months. Magic ought to act a sight faster."

"Perhaps," said Tansy, who didn't see why curses shouldn't bide their time. She had said nothing about the burning of Geoff's card and so far nothing had come of it. But it would…

"Besides," said Kate, chucking the stone from hand to hand, "I worked a healing charm into the grapes I sent."

★ ★ ★

At length Sophie carried her daughter from the pile of blankets up to the cot room. The sheets were already folded back. Calypso's favourite towel was clamped to her cheek, red from the fire's heat. Sophie laid her on the bed. She ran her fingers down the silky brown legs lightly, as fur likes to be stroked. Calypso shivered, yawned pleasurably and lapsed into sleep. The lids that seemed never to close in daylight had set like a half-moon, over eyes already blind and dreaming. Sophie watched her for several minutes. Through a gap between the floorboards a blade of light sliced the room and the din of plates and talk from the room below possessed it. Only occasionally a silence would filter up and the smell of burning ash from the fire. Outside, the sea would toss a plume of spray higher than the cliffs and set a wraith adrift in the tall grasses.

Sophie kissed her daughter and left the room. But she felt suddenly short of breath, and instead of going back to the hall she took the left-hand turning, down the steep back flight to an outer door, and lifted the latch.

The Tor rose before her, unbelievably close. It hung, black as a storm cloud, against the traces of a drowned sun. To her left, the lights of the mainland repeated the constellations above, where her fate was said to be encrypted. To Sophie, the future seemed less than ever in her own control.

When she arrived in Sweetholm she had, for the first time in her life, felt herself to be half a pace ahead of the tide of events. Now things had changed. Dominic had come and was concerning himself with her daughter in ways she did not understand. Of course, she trusted Dominic. Trust came easily to her, as few other things did. But his concerns were not hers. In a noble enough cause she knew that he would sacrifice her and Calypso without hesitation. Himself as well, of course – and that with a kind of fierce pleasure. The whole island might sink under the weight of what Dominic thought was right.

The threads were running through her fingers. Calypso was swimming free. She would lose Calypso now as she had lost Joseph. And all that would be left in her hand was a grief as hard as stone.

9. Joseph

"I thought it might be you."

"I'm sorry to call so late."

Sal waved Dominic into her room, where he sat on the threadbare chaise longue that doubled as Sal's bed. She regarded his awkward courtesy with amusement and said in a plodding voice, "You want some help with your enquiries, officer?"

Dominic did not laugh. He felt exhausted. For the first time it seemed as if the whole business might be too much for him. And now he was reduced to taking long shots, like this with Sal.

"I want to know about Calypso's father," he said.

Sal looked surprised and her long nose twitched. "I suppose I should have guessed…"

"One thing's clear to me. Calypso's real history goes back a long way – long before she was born. I haven't been told the half of it."

Sal sat up a little straighter. "And you're saying this might help her?"

"I hope so." He leaned forward, his hands clasped. "Her power makes her very vulnerable, Sal."

Sal considered. The idea seemed to trouble her. "Sophie

doesn't talk about it much. I don't think she's even told Calypso her father's name…"

"That may have been a mistake. Secrets like that have a way of festering."

Dominic waited.

"I'll admit the fire was a shock," said Sal.

"It could be worse next time."

"I realise that. But – what do you want to know exactly?"

"Whatever might help. Did you like him?"

"Joe? No, not much. But you know what they say about first impressions. I met him when I visited Sophie at the squat in Plinth. Some lanky git playing air guitar, strumming the air and shaking his hair down over his head. Not *simpatico*. Afterwards, though, someone took me aside and told me about him and Sophie. Then I liked him even less. Because a lot of people in that squat were smackheads and I thought he'd drag Sophie down. She wasn't like the rest in that place. She'd only been there two weeks. She was just after an adventure then." Sal looked at Dominic directly for the first time. "She wanted to be like you."

"You're right. She thought my life was glamorous," smiled Dominic.

"At first, I tried to get her away from Joe. Not hard enough. I said she could join me in the Bristol flat, but I knew she'd refuse. I didn't really want some kind of kid sister there, not when I already had Harper to manage. Until afterwards, when I heard about the black magic."

Dominic started. "Sophie did say something about – black magic, did you call it? That's not the word, surely. She told me they used to hold seances. They had an ouija board, I think. Lots of teenagers go through a phase like that. It doesn't come to anything."

"One or two of her friends had studied things more deeply. They saw – *Sophie* saw things that frightened her. I know, you'll say it was the drugs. Well, I don't know what she was on at the time, but there was more to it than chemicals. These things were *probing*. They were trying to feel their way into the circle. And they found a weak link."

Dominic removed a battered box from his shirt pocket and began to fiddle with it unconsciously. Sal recognised the brand.

"I'd never have thought it of you, Dominic. Thanks." She took a cigarette and lit up, drawing deeply so that the next part of her story was draped in smoke.

"The first thing was the sunlight. Sometimes, she said, the sunlight faltered for a moment, as though a flock of birds had flown across it. At night she felt a swarm of fingers work softly on her skin. Her sleep was plagued with voices. Far too many voices – you understand me? Day by day I saw the change in her and in them all. The ones who had been energetic became listless, uninterested. They still drank, but they wouldn't eat anything except the blandest food: white bread, pulses, fat-free yoghurt. At night they would slope out on to the street, or crawl to the beaches and lie there within sound of the surf. As that summer wore on, they spent more and more time at the sea's edge – collecting driftwood for bonfires, sitting out a vigil through the lengthening nights. Sophie got so thin, her skin all smooth, like she was just some wax doll. Some of them would swim, but she always stayed by the fire. She was afraid of the breakers. She said that deep-sea creatures might risk the foreshore by darkness. She began to talk about those bonfires as though they were beacon lights. You think she was crazy? She didn't know what, but something was coming for her. Poor Sophie, she wouldn't even get her feet wet."

"Go on," said Dominic.

"Joe was different – he swam further than anyone. He was a strong swimmer and at night he liked to show it, going beyond the rocks where the rip tides ran. Every night a little further, out towards Sweetholm squatting there in the Channel. If only I could have seen it then, the spell they were all under! The line that was winding them in! But I was on the edge of that group. I put everything down to the dope and the drink, and I had my own troubles with Harper. I couldn't have known what was going to happen, could I?"

"No one could have known," Dominic assured her.

"Not even you, priest man?" smiled Sal. "All the same, I think I'll never forgive myself, even though the end of it was Calypso."

Sal flicked away the ash that had been threatening to fall on to the rug. Slowly, she told Dominic the rest of the story.

★ ★ ★

I was there the night it happened. Harper's dad had shown up and taken the boy for the weekend. He did that once in a while. I wanted to get some sleep, but Sophie more or less pulled me down to the beach. She seemed scared – that night more than ever. She wanted company. Oh, but she couldn't stay away from the sea.

Down on the beach the clouds were bulking out over the water, sixteen shades of grey. I heard thunder in the hills behind the town and the fire panting. Joe tossed in incense. There were half a dozen of us, maybe. Christine and Christian in a huddle, getting through a bottle of spirits. One of the others had brought a book down and started reading it out loud. It began as a book of ghost stories: stories about days that started out happy, but turned into something dark and terrifying. There was something about those stories, something that made your soul sicken. Before I knew what was happening, they were no longer stories. This guy was reading out names, and calling to the spirits of the air, calling on Demogorgon, to all the lords of the deep. And then there really was a burst of lightning right on cue, and the fire sparked just like some horror film, and I was terrified...

And the next thing I knew I was waking up, with a crick in my neck and sand in my socks. The fire was out, but for a fizz where the drizzle damped it down. There was a grudging, early morning light. Christian and Christine still conked out, their fingers clenching sand. A couple of the others, just the same, a bit further from the fire, as if they'd been tossed up like black ashes and dropped. Not us, I thought, it wasn't us they wanted...

And there were Sophie and Joe, tucked up in the one sleeping bag.

Joe was manic that day. No one could say anything to him. He'd swum so far by darkness, threaded caves by touch out in the utter dark, brushed against the scales of living things. He had stayed down for minutes on end, for hours. He was gabbling. As for Sophie, he couldn't keep his hands off her. When they got back to the squat and found they'd lost the key, he punched the door in with his fist. You could see the knuckle marks in the plywood. By rights he should have broken every bone in his hand. But he just laughed and kissed Sophie. Sophie was in a daze. She didn't know what had happened to him.

I wonder if she guessed even then that she was carrying his child?

I saw less of them after that. Some friends of mine offered me work in Kent for a few weeks, so I took Harper apple-picking. Wonderful late-summer days, and Harper running through the trees and gorging, growing taller by the hour. I tried to take snaps of those moments in my mind, to take the imprint of that happiness with me, to hold close to my heart whatever. Even then, the thought of that last night on the beach was niggling at me.

When I came back, I went straight round to the squat. Sophie was there, sitting beside a basket of washing. She'd bring it back wet from the launderette, to save the money for the drier, and now she was about to put it out all round the flat. Except she didn't have the energy to start.

"I brought you some apples," I said and laid my own basket beside hers.

"Thanks," said Sophie. She took one and polished it.

"Where's Joe?" I asked.

She glanced to the bedroom door. "He doesn't come out much now. Not before dark."

When Joe appeared, he was changed too. In the early days he'd gone round naked to the waist, showing off his lean, rock-star torso, the ends of his hair just brushing his chest. Now he covered up, though the weather was still hot. He wasn't pleased to see *me*, that was obvious. He drank water and ate even less than before. Once, when he thought no one was looking, I caught him straining out the cabbage water into a cup and gulping it down. But he hardly spoke at all, just hung round the edges of the room. It was as if they were all in a conspiracy to pretend he wasn't there.

Then the smell began.

At first I thought Sophie had simply taken to lighting more incense than normal. Suddenly every room had two or three joss sticks. But nothing could quite cover up the stink of sea and rotting weed. It was clear too that it came from Joe – Joe, who spent two hours of every day soaking in the bath with the door locked behind him. Sophie knew what was going on, I think. And of course it terrified her – she would admit nothing. Especially with Joe's child growing in her belly.

It was Harper who first saw it, poor mite. The screws on the bolt of the bathroom door were always coming loose and one day he barged in as Joe was shaving. Joe had a towel round his waist and the room was steamed up from the bath he had just left. Harper told me later that for a moment he thought he had stepped into a cave, with the spray drifting through it like bitter smoke. Then something dark had moved towards him out of the smoke. He ran.

"Mum!" he cried. He tumbled down the stairs in his panic, not knowing where I was. He found me in the kitchen with Sophie.

"Mum! Joe has got *scales*!"

I looked quickly at Sophie. Harper clambered on to my lap, turning my head so that I had to look straight at him.

"Joe has got scales growing on him. I saw!"

"Harper, don't talk nonsense."

"But it's true!" he yelled. I could feel him trembling in my arms. "Joe is turning into a *fish*!"

I can't remember what I said to calm him down. Probably I made it into a game, a dressing-up game that Joe was playing. Whether he believed me… Well, I suppose he had to, didn't he? But later, Sophie told me the truth.

"It's a rash," she said. "It started in the small of his back, then spread. Now it's almost covered his shoulders, his stomach too. The skin's all hard and dry. Shiny even – I can see why Harper thought of scales."

Had he been to a doctor? Sophie said he had.

"The GP was no use, he didn't have a clue. Sent Joe to a specialist. I went with him. If I hadn't, I tell you he'd never have gone! Joe was so frightened of doctors, even before this started."

"What did the specialist say?"

"He had a word, a big Latin one. But he said it really meant they didn't know what was going on. It might be a kind of fungal infection, he said. He could have picked it up swimming off the Point."

"Everyone goes swimming there. I never heard of anything like this."

"Not as far out as Joe. Beyond the Point, that's where the town sewage gets pumped out. All kinds of crud. You can probably get your choice of disease out there."

"And that's what you think it is? A fungus?"

"I don't know what to think, Sal! But he's ill, and he's getting worse, and he won't face it! He won't go in for tests, he says, no way!"

I asked her, "Do you love him, Sophie?"

She didn't want to answer that.

"I can't let him go, not the father of my baby."

And the way she said it, I knew it wasn't just Joe she was afraid for.

Joe got worse after that. The rash spread to his hands. He began to wear gloves, grateful for the cold weather when it came. The shopkeepers who stood waiting while he pushed pennies on to the counter with his clumsy, woollen fingers, they must have guessed something was wrong – that he was hiding an awful scar perhaps – but no one asked. Sophie became his protector: she did up his buttons, thought through all the situations that could cause him distress and diverted them.

One night, there were the three of us: me and Joe and Sophie. The two Chrisses and the rest of them, they'd drifted off to the pub, I think. They'd done that a lot lately – Joe unnerved them, of course. The days of those big beach vigils were gone. No more hangers-on staggering through the bonfire smoke or cutting their ankles on sharp stones. Now it was winter, with hail on the skylight and a hungry wind scavenging the seafront. It was just the three of us. The two of *them*, really, because I still lived with Harper a train ride away, and was only visiting for Sophie's sake. Besides, what was happening with Joe I didn't want Harper to see.

Pardon me? No, I don't think it had anything to do with the town sewage. I think we were way beyond that.

"You've got to do this, Joe," I said. "You've got to go back to the specialist. For Sophie's sake, if not for your own. For the child's!"

"That child's nothing to do with me," said Joe for maybe the thousandth time. At first that made me so angry, because everyone knew Sophie would never cheat on him. She'd been about as near a saint as you can get without registering for a halo. If he was denying paternity to get out of paying...

But it wasn't quite that simple. "It's got nothing to do with me," he said, and when I looked at his face, and heard the loss in his voice, I began to understand. He was *lonely*. He no longer felt attached to anyone, any human being at all. Sure, Sophie stuck by him and he let her do it, but he looked back at her as if she were part of a different species. When she scurried around him it was like one of those birds that hop inside a crocodile's mouth picking insects out of its teeth. I felt he might snap those jaws shut any time. "It's got nothing to do with me." That was a cry of despair, surely?

And a plea of Not Guilty, too. That's only just occurred to me – knowing what I know now. I think he guessed what had happened to Calypso. He wanted us to understand it wasn't his fault. He hadn't meant to do it. He hadn't meant to curse his daughter.

I'd better get back to the night he disappeared. It was November. We hadn't been to the sea for weeks. For weeks the mizzle had been fumbling the latch with its slack fingers, house to house. Warm rain from the south and I couldn't bear it. Now, suddenly, there was this winter hail and the wind gusting in from Archangel. So you can imagine what we said when Joe suggested a walk on the beach – it was mad! You might as well have argued with a stone. Joe was almost crippled: the callused skin had swallowed him from his thighs to the nape of his neck. Only Sophie could bear to touch him. She said you could feel the muscles gliding under your fingertips: it was like touching a snake.

"I've got to go now," he said as if he was under a spell.

So he went alone. Sophie tried to follow, but could not keep up, and he had a trick of disappearing. By the seafront, she found herself kicking up sand at the top of the stone steps to the beach. She looked at the whole bay, the dark cliffs beyond the town, the flares from the Plant and, across the Channel, Sweetholm and the dim lights hemming the far coast. The Victorian pleasure walks, all the Victorian things. Then, down to the beach itself. For a second she had him as he slipped beneath the water.

His clothes were flung here and there, and when she lifted his shirt there was a tinkle of skin scales falling to the sand. A breeze blew them up again and inland. She caught just one. It's all that she still has of Calypso's father.

Days passed. Long nights, too, and no sign of Joe. On the third day, Sophie presented herself at the local police station. She had come to report a missing person. They made her fill out a form. She showed them the clothes, which she'd brought in a carrier bag. She shouldn't have done that, they said; it would contaminate them. The clothes were evidence.

They thought it might be suicide at first, but no body ever turned up and no note either. After that they changed their tune, especially when they knew he was the father of her child. He'd done a runner, they said, to avoid paying for support.

But by that time Sophie wasn't listening. She wanted you, Dominic, her big brother, who always knew what to do. It took days to find you: the Seminary had no idea. It was the time the plague broke out and everything was chaotic. But at last she got her one phone call, a felon's ration of sympathy and advice. What did you say to her, I wonder? You couldn't come, of course – the world had need of you. You had an opinion though.

When I found Sophie later she had already dried her tears.

"I'm keeping this baby," she told me.

"Then let me take you back to Bristol, at least, where I can look after you."

"I've got everything I need here."

"Sophie, you haven't."

At last she packed her bag and we caught the train to Temple Meads. At my flat she filled two shelves with her belongings and another with baby things she picked up second-hand. Joe's carrier bag was still with the cops. It's probably been incinerated by now.

Oh, I didn't like him. I said that at the beginning, but he didn't deserve what happened to him. No one could.

PART TWO

THE TOR

10. On the Beach

Tansy took a brush with hard bristles and scrubbed the board, while her mother rehung the bedroom curtains.

"The dust of ages was in this lot."

Hilary had found a carpet beater in the outside toilet. She had spent ten minutes flinging dust up from the line in the yard and come in red-faced and spluttering. The day before, she had decided to wash the doorstep, perhaps for the first time in her life. She had even been weeding Uncle John's carrots, a daunting quarter-acre of them. "Once begun is half done," she explained, rolling her sleeves. Everything she did spoke of her enthusiasm for the place, a gale strong enough to flatten whole groves of shallow-rooted habit.

"Don't you think you're overdoing it a bit?" Tansy asked at the end of the second week. "This is meant to be a holiday as well, you know."

"Oh, I know, I know," said her mother, but did not break her stride.

Tansy was pleased, of course, that her mother (who had been so sceptical about their Sweetholm summer) was happy here. It hurt her too, because she could not share that happiness and she wanted to share everything with Hilary. Weeding, watering, scraping dirt from floors, all gave her mother far more than the wholesome satisfaction of a job well done. A secret pleasure, in fact. Almost, Tansy thought, as if Hilary were in love with the place.

"How much polish can a chest of drawers need?" Geoff asked testily one day as he saw Hilary setting to with the beeswax once again.

"Oh, but it likes it, Geoff, it's so *beautiful*," said Hilary without looking up. "The way it *glows*."

"You've never taken half this trouble over the real antiques we have in Bristol," Geoff complained.

He's jealous, Tansy thought. Jealous of a chest of drawers – imagine!

And then: I wonder if that's why she's doing it?

Only the phone calls upset Hilary. Twice more the phone had rung and Hilary had answered to a silence at the other end: number withheld. Had it been Gloria? When challenged, Geoff had indeed looked furtive, but that might be no more than habit. Tansy, for one, felt she had to trust him.

Trust was a very delicate thing, thought Tansy. The thread of trust, once snapped, might unravel a whole life. If she hadn't burnt that playing card in the Cursing Candle then Geoff and Gloria would never have got together. Two families would not now be tottering and her friendship with Kate would have survived.

Tansy had no doubt that these events had begun with her. The curse had run through their lives like a corrosive acid, seeking the lowest level. Every day she saw her father squirm under a guilt that was not truly his, while her mother's happiness seemed to lie in building a life without him. But somehow it was impossible to talk about this with either of them. The affair was over after all, the storm weathered. They had come to Sweetholm to forget and start again. Besides, her parents would not believe her. Tansy knew how they scoffed at her interest in magic. So she was left alone, with only the truth for company.

Sweetholm, for good or ill, was changing them all. As Hilary dug herself into the land, so Geoff became more detached from it – and from everything else. His conversation began to take on a philosophical flavour. A simple enquiry after biscuits was liable to turn into a meditation on the worth and meaning of life. He took long walks over the moor alone, mulling these questions over. For her part, Tansy had begun to dislike her new home. Every time she looked out of her window it was to catch a glimpse of Davy Jones labouring in their back garden – an act of neighbourliness it would be ungrateful to resent, though she itched to. The paths to the cliffs were never entirely empty, though the wayfarers Tansy saw there kept their distance, and their faces were perpetually muffled against sun or wind. In the Haven she felt that the islanders – how few, how old they seemed! – wished her elsewhere. And she was lonely.

Her chores complete, Tansy set off for the beach, where she had agreed to meet Harper. The sky rippled overhead. Even the sky was strange to her here. It would not stay still, not even on cloudless days, not for an instant. A subtle curtain of light was draped across the island. The sea would flick it up playfully or spit at it like fat in a pan. Today, a shower could be seen approaching, ponderous and slow as a desert caravan.

As she searched for shelter, she noticed properly for the first time that the heath was not deserted. Up on a ridge of higher ground a group of walkers was making its purposeful way in the direction of the Tor. There were three of them. No – four, it seemed, as they strung out in single file on a narrow portion of the ridge. In the smudged rain-light Tansy could not distinguish faces or even the colour of their clothes.

She opened her mouth to call. If she had missed her path to the bay, perhaps they could set her right. But a shyness overcame her and a series of trivial, off-putting thoughts dribbled through her mind. They might be too far off to hear. They were probably visitors to Sweetholm themselves. Perhaps they did not even speak English. And by now sunlight was avalanching down the Tor towards her. In two minutes the shower would have scudded south, to the grassy peninsula from which she had first peered at Sweetholm through a telescope.

She found Harper on the beach. He was further down the coast today, on the island's sole stretch of sand. The tide was at its lowest and the beach curled out in a spit further along. The very end of the spit was hazed by mist and the pebble-roll of the waves was a rumour of echo and delay. Nearer, she could see sandpipers and oystercatchers searching out food. Harper was digging too, lazily intent in the way she was beginning to recognise. Dressed in dungarees and wellingtons, with his hair tied back, he was wedging the spade in the sand and sifting it quickly for lugworms. The sand was dotted with lugworm casts, coiled like cobras.

Behind him Calypso stood devotedly guarding a bucket. Tansy was startled at that. She had not seen Calypso since that day with the camper van, almost three weeks ago. Harper and Tansy had met in various places on the island since, but for reasons of his own he had not invited her back to the Manor. Calypso was caped and hooded, and immobile except when Harper moved along the beach. Then she would shuffle a little distance after him. Calypso had her back to Tansy, but it was a word from Calypso that made Harper look up and spy her among the rocks.

"Come to help?" he called.

Tansy joined them. She peered into Calypso's bucket. Calypso held it out solemnly for her inspection.

"You're helping Harper, are you?" Tansy asked. She was unsure how to address Calypso, but felt that to ignore her altogether might be unwise. Calypso gave the ghost of a nod.

"She's shy with strangers," Harper said matter-of-factly. He took up his spade and dug again.

"People really pay you for those things?" Tansy asked, looking with disgust at the sandy tube of flesh. "Who do you sell them to?"

"The anglers up on the harbour at the Haven. Day trippers mostly. They like a live bait."

"You're quite an entrepreneur, aren't you?" said Tansy. "Just how many of these schemes have you got?"

Harper smiled. "I keep busy. It's not really about money, is it?"

"No?"

"Sal likes me to fill up the days somewhere healthy. I enjoy it too. And then there's Sophie. I'm looking after Calypso for her. She says it's safer to keep her moving."

"He's still watching us," Calypso said.

Calypso's gaze had not moved from the streaked sand. But, as if she had placed the thought in their minds, both Harper and Tansy found themselves looking up to the cliff top behind her. The sun blinded them. Even so they could see the movement of a man's figure as it loped along the cliff's edge and the long, curved stick it carried. Tansy beat back a sudden impulse to dive to the ground and hide.

Harper stared at the place a good few seconds, shrugged and set back to work. "It's nothing."

Tansy drew Harper aside. "Listen, Harper. I know it's against your religion to give a straight answer, but is Calypso in some kind of trouble?"

"It pays to be careful. Calypso's special, you've seen that for yourself. Look at her hands, the seal-down on her feet, the webbed toes. Look at her eyes. You'll never see her blink. Of course she draws attention. But if that was all…"

"The van – what about that?"

"Exactly." Harper paused, with his spade balanced in his hand. "She's never done anything quite like that before. But Calypso has always *known* things. She's always been able to see into locked rooms, dark places. Recently, she's been able to move objects too. I've seen a ladle drop into the sink when no one was in touching distance. You'll come into a room and find a pair of scissors dancing on their points. When she realises you're there, they fall. She's got no real control, you see." He levered the spade into the sand again, grunting as he put his weight on to his left foot. "Sometimes she can tell the future."

Tansy considered a moment. "But who are you all afraid of? Is someone trying to get hold of Calypso?"

"All I know is, Sophie and Sal have been getting twitchy since spring. You never heard of an island without treasure on it, did you? Well, Calypso's the treasure on Sweetholm. She needs guarding."

Tansy looked back at Calypso, who was sketching cities in the sand with a stick. Despite the half-human roundness of her eyes and the concealment of the long shift dress, heavy now around the hem with a fringe of sand and water, Calypso was an ordinary child in every way that mattered. And beautiful: it was easy to see why so many clustered to the task of protecting her. Tansy felt that tug strongly too. To be a magical child. To straddle two worlds and belong to neither, see both. It was dizzying and pitiable. Tansy no longer wished for it.

Calypso had dropped the stick to poke her fingers into mussel shells, make shell castanets and twine her hair. She was absorbed in her own game, like any four-year-old. But now and then she would tense, as Tansy had seen animals tense at the rustling of the grass at their back. Then she would look up to the cliff-top path, where there was nothing to be seen. Or to the shingle causeway or the sea. To the sea, increasingly.

"I'm the Queen of London!" cried Calypso, standing on a stone. She pelted them with handfuls of glittering sand and soon Tansy forgot her fears in mounting an assault on the Stone of London, from which London's Queen was borne off giggling, slung like a sprawled lobster on Harper's back.

"What sort of place is the Manor?" Tansy asked Harper as they helped Calypso back up the cliff path. "I've heard talk about a cult."

"Have you?" said Harper shortly. "No prizes for guessing where."

"What do you mean?"

"All that poison they spout in the Haven will do for us in the end." He climbed on, clanking the bucket, and helping Calypso over the higher rocks.

"So Gerard Winstanley hasn't got you handing over all your worldly goods?"

"What goods? You're wrong about Mr Winstanley. He's a kind of *scientist*, really. But – they haven't come up with a name for what he does. He calls it the Cure of Souls. He's a shrink, a guru – maybe a magician. He keeps chickens too. Grows a lovely Brussels sprout. And of course there are the computers. But it's all about one thing really. He wants to make people well and he knows the old ways won't do it. Not religion, and even science is hitting the skids. Hooked up to the Money Engine, see?"

Tansy could tell from the way he said it that the last phrase came with capital letters. Probably the Money Engine was some slogan Harper had picked up from his mother or Gerard Winstanley. Easy to talk that way when you had plenty yourself.

"Why don't you come and see?" said Harper unexpectedly.

"Now?" asked Tansy.

"Once a week we all have a meal together. It's a kind of custom. Why don't you come this afternoon? Sal won't mind. No one will."

"Will there be enough food?" Tansy wondered. Her own mother had a very precise idea of what constituted one person's rations. But when Tansy remembered the set-up at the Manor it was obvious that things would be different there. Not for them the boxed and frozen meals-for-three of Bristol. They'd be ladling lentils from a communal cauldron, probably, or raking potatoes from the embers of a camp fire, and the more the merrier.

"What's the matter? Scared you'll catch something?"

"No, no, of course I'll come," smiled Tansy. "I'm curious anyway."

"Listen, I'm asking you as a friend, not a journalist," warned Harper. "No interrogations, see, if people act a bit—"

"Yes?"

"A bit not what you're used to." Harper was already ten yards ahead, and this last remark was flung back over his shoulder.

Tansy followed, surprised at his sudden vehemence. "I didn't mean—"

"You may be curious, but people aren't curiosities, OK?"

He stopped abruptly to let her catch up.

"I know," she said as she drew level. "I just meant I'd be pleased to meet them."

Harper paused. "Sorry," he said at last. "It's a touchy subject. All those long stares we get from the islanders have made me a bit sensitive. I only hope…"

"What?"

Harper gave a rueful grin. "Nothing. I hope you've got a healthy appetite, that's all."

11. Queenie

The stew was spicy, rich in red and green vegetables. Loaves of dark bread were distributed across two trestle tables. It was Harper's mother, Sal, who served them all, not from a cauldron – not quite – but from a vast saucepan that sat on the range. The wooden bowls with their wooden spoons were carried by a quiet man called Albert who seemed unsure what to do with them until relieved by the hungry diners. At length, however, everyone was served and at that point Gerard Winstanley rose to his feet. Tansy noticed how quickly the conversation faded around her. Winstanley cleared his throat.

"On these occasions it has become customary for me to speak a few words," he began in his most silvery voice. "And I hope that our guests—" (here he smilingly acknowledged Tansy, Dominic and – to Tansy's surprise – Davy Jones, whom she was finding it impossible to escape) "—will excuse me if I say a kind of grace.

"Grace, they called it in the old days," Winstanley continued. "God, having given freely of his bounty, was to be thanked. More than that, he was to be asked for further gifts – the gifts of humility and gratitude. Gifts that our self-glorifying age would scarcely recognise as such!"

There were murmurs of agreement around the room.

"Alas, the God of traditional religion has long since withered on the vine. We can no longer hope to find a God outside ourselves – but we can still search within. And here lies the difficulty. For in each of us is a Babel of desires, selfish demands, lusts. How, from this confusion, shall we distinguish the still small voice that will guide us truly?"

Somewhere to Tansy's left came the sound of a chair being pushed back.

Winstanley raised an admonitory finger. "Think again of that small word, grace. It is a word with many meanings. It means God's blessing and forgiveness, yes; but also the quality that blessing bestows on the one who receives it. We see a graceful dancer, we hear a musician playing graceful music – but we can also say that certain lives are *lived* with grace. And while the dancer or musician may live ugly lives, a life lived with grace will always be both beautiful *and* good. It is indeed through such lives that we see the beauty proper to all true goodness. Therefore, we might do worse than ask: Will this action, this word, this thought, add to the grace that is in the world? Or will it add to the world's ugliness? For of this at least I am certain – there is no ugliness in the divine."

Tansy heard little of this speech, being engrossed by the sight of Calypso making doughballs out of the bread and threading them on a string to make herself a necklace. But as Gerard Winstanley finished, she was aware of a movement beside the door. She looked up to see Davy Jones leaving the room. His face was thunder.

"What was *he* doing here?" She nudged Harper, next to her at the table.

Sal overheard. "Davy only came to fix the lights," she said. "Gerard Winstanley coaxed him into staying for the Fellowship Meal. Typical Winstanley."

"He didn't seem to enjoy it much," said Mike.

"Davy's chapel, born and bred," Sal said. "He wouldn't appreciate having God struck from the record."

"He always seems so easy-going," remarked Tansy.

"The guy's a loony," said the one called Mike, before adding with false piety, "though in him, too, divine qualities endure."

"Yes, Mike," said Sophie. "Even in you, they do."

Calypso had her toys, like any child. A length of sky-blue towelling accompanied her to her bed each night and only sweets or the lure of a piggyback from Harper were enough to win its passport to the wash. Her favourite, though, was her rag doll, a rhapsody in frill and calico, with smudgy ink eyes that stared incessantly. Tansy found her playing with it after dinner, or rather regarding with complacency its unquestioning smile and florid cheeks. An upturned hi-fi box had recently become the doll's home.

"What's she called?" asked Tansy.

It was a risky question, leading as it probably would to getting down on all fours and spending half an hour in some pink pre-school fantasy. But it seemed important to be Calypso's ally – to understand her. And she *was* curious, and a little afraid too. So, when Calypso did not appear to have heard her question, she repeated, "What's she called, your doll?"

"Queenie," Sophie replied, overhearing. "That's right, isn't it, Calypso?"

Calypso looked up solemnly. "That's what *most* people call her," she explained. "But it's not her real name."

"No? What is her name then?" asked Tansy.

"I've got her Certificate," Calypso announced and, fumbling inside the hi-fi house, she produced a much-folded piece of paper, which had been printed to look like parchment. *Certificate of Adoption*, it was headed. Calypso had filled the spaces for the parents' names, printing her own in both with laborious care. But

95

the space for the baby's name had been left blank.

"There's nothing written there."

"You want to know who Queenie really is?" Calypso asked Tansy, her eyes even wider than normal. And she put her arms round Tansy's neck and whispered loudly, "It's a secret!"

"Well then, I'll have to guess! Like in the story."

"You'll never get it!"

"Let me see... Is it Hyssop? Or Muchpenny? Or Ambergrise?"

"No!" exclaimed Calypso in an ecstasy of contempt.

"Mooncalf? Dodder? Twitchet?"

"No, silly!"

"Then I give up."

"Then you'll never know," said Calypso, a little sadly. She turned back to her doll.

But later Calypso beckoned her closer. She looked over to make sure the adults were still busy with their own affairs at the trestle table, then said, "She's called Bridget. But you mustn't tell!"

"I won't," promised Tansy gravely.

"If you do..." warned Calypso – and at once Tansy felt a fluttering in her abdomen and all the hanging pans rattled ominously against the wall. A second later a dragon's roar scorched the house, hammering at the windows with a sudden clamour.

Tansy gave a small scream. The adults at their table looked over.

"Military exercise," explained Winstanley. "Get them all the time here."

Sure enough, outside the window a pair of dark green jets were skimming the Channel. The pans stopped rattling and the trestle-table conversation turned for a while to a murmur of complaint against the planes.

"They wouldn't do it in London – they'd stop tomorrow if it was Islington windows being shaken."

"As if guns solved anything."

But when Tansy looked back at Calypso, she was still holding her finger to her lips and nodding. Tansy saw that for Calypso those planes belonged not to the Air Force but to her. She had conjured them, to thunder out a warning and depart.

"Bridget talks to me," said Calypso, "when I'm falling asleep. She tells me stories about my daddy."

"Yes?"

"He's a farmer, did you know? And a policeman. But mostly he catches fish."

"What a busy man!"

"He doesn't need a net – he just reaches down into the water and scoops them out with his hand. That's what Bridget says."

"How does Bridget know all this?" asked Tansy.

"Bridget knows everything," said Calypso proudly. "She's very clever. But sometimes I have to be cross with her, because she won't let me sleep. Then I say, 'You're not real, Bridget, you're nothing but a stuffed rag! If you don't let me sleep, I'll unpick you!'" Calypso was in raptures at the sheer naughtiness of the suggestion. Her doll, crooked in her arm, smiled broadly.

Calypso crawled off with Bridget and her beloved towel to the chimney corner where, amid a pile of crocheted blankets, she had established a den. Tansy found Harper talking to Dominic at the far end of the room. Dominic, staring gloomily at his uneaten meal, seemed lost in some meditation of his own. "When did you realise you were a Healer?" Harper was asking.

Dominic barely glanced at him, for the question was familiar. "Long ago. When I was eight years old. Sophie was hardly born then."

He took a breath and plunged into a pool of deep memory.

"I saw a car smash into a dog, hit and run. This little terrier was lying there trying to breathe, just whimpering. But the wheels had crushed its chest and the ribs were broken. There was no one else nearby. Eight years old and there I was, laying my hands on that animal's head and talking gibberish, and I could feel the warmth trickling out through my fingers first and then pouring down. It was like I was bathing that dog in liquid gold. I could almost see it streaming from my skin, mending bone and blood and making the poor animal live. The dog got to its feet in the end and staggered off. And I was the one left crippled under the shade of the privet hedge: exhausted and knowing that from that moment I was no longer my own creature. I'd been dedicated. No person, no ambition would ever mean so much. I knew it even then."

Dominic got to his feet and walked to the door of the yard, where his van still stood caked in the blackened mud. Tansy saw his shoulders sigh. "And that's the way it has been."

"That must have been about the time the Disasters began," said Tansy, working it out. "The Red Leprosy, the floods in Polynesia."

"Began? Oh, I think they'd been waiting to happen long before that," said Dominic. "When a cloth grows threadbare you see what lies beneath it, that is all."

Harper looked puzzled. "How can something like that be *waiting*?"

Dominic seemed relieved to talk. "The psychologists have known it for years. Beneath each rational mind lies another: deeper, darker, older. That is where the nightmare demons live. Our precious reason is just a side-effect – and so easily overthrown!" He lowered his voice as if he were approaching a secret. "What only the theologians know is that the World too has a mind. Its conscious thoughts are time, space, gravity – the laws of physics. They seem to be everywhere we look, regular and predictable. But the dreams of the World Soul too are demon-haunted. And, as with human minds, the demons may escape into waking life." Dominic blew into his hands. "That is when magic begins."

"Mr Winstanley won't talk about magic," said Harper. "He says it's a cop-out."

Dominic shook his head. "Just look around you – every day it's happening more. The World Soul grows neurotic. Twenty years ago, the Red Leprosy did not exist. There were no Healers: now there are hundreds of us. There are other events I have heard of. A smack of madness in all of them."

"But why should all this be happening now?" asked Tansy suddenly. "What's changed?"

"The Asklepians have their theories," said Dominic, turning to her for the first time. "Some say it's a punishment, for the way we've treated the earth and the arrogance behind it. But I believe the world is reverting. One hears tales of an ancient time, an Age of Enchantment. I think that something of this kind has happened before."

"Something of *what* kind?"

He looked at her as if she were obtuse. "The powers of the underworld are waking," he told her. "Call them demons or call them gods, as you wish. They are trying to claw their way back into the universe."

"But how?" asked Tansy. She found Dominic's intensity alarming, but whether it was Dominic himself or the things he was saying that disturbed her most was hard to determine under those blue, fanatic eyes.

"Through belief, to begin with. Without belief they are barely more than nothing – and worship is the sweetest belief of all. But once they are established, they will make themselves known in ways that are more… *objective*."

"So what can we do about it?" said Tansy in dismay.

Dominic put his hand on her shoulder. She thought she

could feel the warmth of healing flow down through her shirt, through skin and muscle into her blood, strong and comforting. But Dominic's face, when she looked back up at it, was as pale and cold as a statue's.

"Pray," said the Asklepian. "Practise compassion. Have courage. Pray, most of all."

At length, Harper moved away – Tansy saw him talking to Sal at one point, then leaving with the one they called Albert. Tansy found herself alone. The people at the trestle table beyond the stone flags were all so comfortable in each other's company, it seemed, such a happy circle. Suddenly, she was shy and lonely again. For the first time in hours she remembered her parents, and with a pang of guilt remembered, too, a promise to help her father with the fencing that afternoon. Somehow three hours had elapsed since she'd entered the Manor. Sweetholm time ran fast, like the tide. It could carry you away with it.

It was Gerard Winstanley who noticed her preparing to leave.

"Tansy, we've neglected you!" he called, moving towards her with his hand outstretched. He saw her anxiety and smiled. "Relax – no one here is going to eat you."

"After all, we're neighbours," said Sophie.

"I ought to be going," Tansy began. "My mum and dad will be wondering—"

"How do you like the island life?" said another woman. "A change from the city, I should think."

"A change from teaching, too, is hoeing carrots. I've a wonderful lotion for a sore back – be sure and tell your mother."

Tansy stammered, "She hasn't said anything about a sore back."

"Then she can't be working hard enough! The soil up on John Robinson's place is thinner than Gerard's hair."

They smiled back at her. A row of smiles, all welcoming.

Were they too welcoming, Tansy wondered? She remembered again what she had heard about such places. How they took you at your lowest and gave you unconditional love, brimming over until your soul quailed and you said in your secret heart, "I do! I love you back!"

And that was the end of you, girl.

But there was Sal, sensible woman. There was Harper, out in the yard. A dreamer, sure (who knew what any of them *really* believed?) but his own person. He wouldn't do or say anything unless he saw good reason.

"I'm sorry, I made a promise," she said.

On her way home that afternoon Tansy made another decision, one that seemed somehow connected. She would tell Geoff about the Cursing Candle. She had let him carry the burden of guilt alone for too long: it wasn't fair. She would confess, he would forgive her and the curse she had laid on him would blow itself out harmlessly against the fortress of their love and trust. So that would be an end to all suspicion on the island. And they would start living gracefully again.

12. Revelation

Cold. Cold. My hand feels nothing. And there is no light neither, till I light a match and watch him burn, make a finger cathedral as he flares up on that wall. Quickly I light the tallows, two score of them, to stake my yard of holiness. They form a shrine about St Brigan, who has come to bless Sweetholm. To you, Saint, I pledge my service.

Brigan of the bright face, do you accuse me? Have I been lacking in my service? But not in my devotion! Your bones should be gilded, stand above the canons' perpetual chanting, be adored to the sound of choir and organ. Such was the strain of our fathers, which so pleased you that you made their island a second paradise, a haven for the sea-tossed and a pilgrimage for the holy.

And now it is abased. Your sacred ground is overgrown, the immortal flame has been left to gutter and die. Even your name is turned to the glory of other gods. Shepherdess, healer, seer, smith: tell me, how shall I be justified?

Brigan looked down at her disciple from the niche in the limestone. Her limbs were born of three separate islands. Her face was a mosaic of limpet, mussel, crab; her hair the sad lovers' weed of sea willow and black mourning. The devotion pleased her, though, who had been so long a prisoner of memory. A fanatic kneeled before her image once again. She was loved and the power of love coursed through her. She made the tallow candles flicker. She smiled and the fragments of crab shell touched and curved upwards. Gruesome to any but the one beholder, whom – *o altitudo!* – it pitched into an ecstatic faint.

When Davy Jones awoke, the candles were extinguished. He no longer felt cold, though, as he lit another match to lead him to the cave's entrance. Indeed, he felt only joy – a light-headed joy. Out of all sinful humanity, St Brigan had chosen him to sanctify her island. Through him the pollution of unbelief would be cleansed and Sweetholm led back mildly as a lamb to the fold. He even knew how. Calypso would be the means – Calypso, whose nature was to span two worlds, as lightning spans earth and heaven. From her the love and glory of St Brigan would shoot forth, in all its annihilating power.

The way out of the cave was through a small opening above his head, which he could reach only by climbing a rope. As he swarmed up it, he was still only half-conscious of himself. He emerged into the light, a fresh salt breeze licking his face. He was near a cliff top and before him the waves were cresting white. The sea had two voices: its own and the mumbling echo trapped in the rock under his feet. Having made certain that he was unobserved, Davy Jones stooped to untie the rope, which he had fixed to a nearby elder tree. Years of onshore wind had beaten the elder down, so that its branches gave shelter and concealment to Brigan's cave. In addition Davy Jones was now carefully pulling a thorny barrier of low bushes around the entrance. A person might have stood just inches away and been quite unaware of the holiness hard by.

His duties complete, Davy Jones put the coiled rope over his shoulder and set off for the Haven. He could see by the sun that his shop would soon be due to open, so he walked a little faster. He wanted to be in good time for the mainland trade.

13. Good Fences

"That should hold it."

Geoff slapped the fence post and stepped back to admire his achievement. Two fresh planks ran parallel to the sloping ground and eight nails shone. Even the Jacob's sheep looked impressed. "I'd like to see them get past *that* without a stepladder."

"It'll do," agreed Tansy.

"Thanks for your help, love. We make a good team."

"All I did was hold a piece of wood in position!"

"And you made it look so easy," flattered Geoff. "Which is always a sign of real talent, you know."

Tansy returned her father's half-mocking smile. That was one of the things about Geoff Robinson that so irritated Hilary – the way he could never say anything (praise or blame) quite *straight*. A little escape clause was always included – a sliver of irony, a hint of exaggeration. Yet Tansy could remember a time when Hilary had not minded this habit. They had joked about it in an easy, teasing sort of way.

This reminded her of something she had meant to ask weeks ago. "Why does Mum keep making cracks about you being brought up in the country? I thought you were from darkest Sheffield."

"I am, really," said Geoff, searching for the thermos. "But me and John, after our mother died, we lived with my grandparents for a year. Till your Grandpa remarried, I suppose. They had a few acres near Lancaster." He unscrewed the thermos lid and poured her tea in a shallow plastic cup. "Sheep and pigs."

"I didn't know," said Tansy, and was surprised that she hadn't. "Mum shouldn't make fun of you," she added thoughtfully. "Not about that."

"She doesn't mean it," said Geoff in his bland, equivocal way.

Tansy spat and gagged. "But this tea's too sweet!"

"Sorry," laughed Geoff. "It's the Davy Jones influence. He won't drink anything with less than six sugars."

Four sugars! thought Tansy, running her tongue over furred teeth. I counted them. More exaggeration!

Clearing the ground next to the fence meant that there was now a pile of dead bracken to burn, as well as the old planks. Geoff and Tansy wheeled it to the garden in a barrow and Geoff set to work building a bonfire, while Tansy (remembering what Harper had said about the island grass) filled buckets from the standpipe, just in case. When she returned she found Geoff half-buried, pushing a wad of paper under some rotten wood at the base of the pile.

"You want to do the honours, Tansy?"

He passed her his windproof lighter. Tansy knelt and burrowed down, careful of her eyes under the tangle of stem and branch. There was a little cavity there, with its own atmosphere of sap and crazed light. Her flame touched the newspaper and Tansy saw a printed photograph crease, then split and curl down. She stared. Fire scuttled up the dry twigs and ran down like water.

"Tansy! Come out of there!" Geoff was shouting.

Tansy pulled back in panic. As she stood up, she found the ends of her hair singed – a little. She hardly noticed. It was the newspaper photo that had terrified her. The photo had not been of Geoff, of course. But, in the moment before the flames took it, that heavy-browed face had seemed to look up at her in surprise – in guilt and alarm. The way Geoff was looking now.

"I'm sorry, I shouldn't have asked you," he said. "With your hair loose – it's my fault."

"Dad!"

"I'll get your mum to trim it. Half an inch should do."

"Dad! Listen to me!"

Geoff stopped, puzzled. "What is it, love?"

The back of Tansy's throat was dry. Yellow smoke was curling up through the bonfire, sinuous and opaque. It snaked between the rotten planks and choked the fleeing insects as they ran. Below it, the fire sat cracking its knuckles.

"Listen," she said, walking towards her father. "There's something you've got to know."

14. The West Walkers

"So what did your dad say?" said Harper.

"Not much," Tansy replied and wished he hadn't asked her.

It was the next day. Tansy and Harper were on Gander's Head, a bulge in the cliff on the Plinth side of Sweetholm. Its clear view of the Channel had prompted the army to build an anti-aircraft placement there in the Second World War. The concrete bunker, the girders, the wafers of rusting iron in the grass were all still there. They seemed more remote than any medieval ruin. Wondering why they unnerved her, Tansy realised that it was because they had not been vandalised. Not sprayed, not swung on. Sweetholm, she felt, was not quite natural.

"The island has never done well for long," Harper agreed. "It's too barren. Not that it's a desert island either. They found Viking pottery here, Roman, older…"

"You'd think they'd learn," said Tansy.

"Here, look at this." Harper was holding a stick. Silently he approached a sheet of corrugated iron that was lying nearby. Using the end of the stick he hooked the metal and flipped it up. Three blue-grey shapes slithered with alarming speed into the grass and were gone.

Tansy shrieked – then felt immediately ashamed of her own

squeamishness. More so when she looked up at Harper's grinning face.

"You idiot! Are you trying to get us bitten?"

"They were slow worms, not snakes! Oh, you should see your expression!"

"*Slow* worms? What a ridiculous name…"

But now she wanted to find the lizards again. To hold one, just to show Harper. They thrashed about in the grass for a few minutes, evicting beetles and spiders. Tansy began to enjoy herself.

But they didn't find any slow worms. Eventually, they collapsed, a little breathlessly, into silence. The hours stretched blankly to the horizon.

Harper asked, "Do you think your mum's forgiven your dad?"

"I don't know," said Tansy shortly.

That morning Tansy had told Harper part of her home story. The affair, the trial of a summer on Sweetholm. The Cursing Candle too. In fragments at first, and then the whole story had come out, till she hadn't known where to stop and had said too much – even down to her decision to confront her father. Harper had listened in that open way of his and said nothing at all. Tansy had been relieved at that. But her story was still clearly rumbling round in his head and issuing in occasional abrupt questions like this one.

"You haven't told me how your dad reacted," Harper added.

"He told me not to worry my head over it," said Tansy briefly. "He was probably right."

Harper looked hurt. "Don't clam up now, Tansy," he pleaded. "It isn't fair."

Tansy turned on him with sudden hostility. "You're an expert on fair, are you?"

Harper shrugged and continued to dissect a scarlet pimpernel. "You know what Gerard Winstanley calls secrets?"

"I suppose you'll tell me."

"Splinters. Splinters under the skin. That's why it hurts whenever you touch anyone."

Tansy did not look at him. "Your mate Winstanley's got all the answers, hasn't he?"

"Not all," said Harper. "I just think it would do you good to tell."

But Tansy could not tell. How could she, when Geoff had made her feel like a little child again? She remembered the look on his face, the quick transitions from guilt, disbelief and embarrassment through to laughter.

Then: "Hell's bells, Tansy! Is that really what's been worrying you all these weeks?" He had tossed down the pitchfork with which he had begun feeding the bonfire and hugged her. And she had cried and laughed with him because not telling had been such a tension within her, and telling in the end had been so easy. The curse had disappeared as soon as it was named, blown away in the woodsmoke.

Still she had needed to be sure. "But, Dad, remember what happened to poor old Mr Podgery—"

"Love, that animal had been living on borrowed time for months. As for Carol Sage, her accident was nobody's fault but her own – skateboarding in the dark like that. What did she expect?" Geoff sounded quite censorious.

"You really think so?"

"I do. Besides," he added a moment later, "you *couldn't* have been responsible for me and Gloria."

Tansy frowned. "Why not?"

"Not if this escapade with the cards happened last November. Did I understand that right?"

"Yes."

"There you are then. We'd been seeing each other for six months by then!"

"Pardon me?"

"At least. It was a good six months earlier we got together. Didn't you know?"

Tansy's brain had gone thuddingly numb. "No – no, I didn't know anything."

"So put this silly thought out of your head. If you start making yourself responsible for other people's actions, you'll have the whole world on your conscience." He put his finger under her chin and pulled it up. "Do you see that, cherub? That way madness lies. The affair was my fault, not yours."

"Yes. I see that," she answered dully.

"Then let's put it behind us, shall we? That's why we came to Sweetholm in the first place, wasn't it? To start again?"

Tansy gazed at him. His voice, his smile. He was shocked, she could tell, that she had been nursing such guilt all this time. He was anxious to make it right. But his words did not touch her. It was only by an effort that she could bring herself to look at him. She did not feel relief any more, just a smouldering, charcoal anger and a new unease she could not yet name.

Even then she had been aware of it. Perhaps it was the way Geoff kept moving in and out of focus when she was with him, the shadow that hovered just behind him or settled blurrily on his skin, where the bonfire smoke was thickest. A shadow that was already in his face and voice.

Harper was talking to her. "Would you like to stay on Sweetholm, Tansy?"

They had been working their way around Gander's Head and now found themselves abruptly at a stay, with only the sea before them. Tansy gasped at the sudden absence.

"It's a black pit," she whispered, peering down.

Harper looked appraisingly at the savage rocks below, the dark water. "I'd love to abseil down there," he said. "There are caves. You can see them from the ferry."

A huge wave crashed into the cliff. Seventy feet above, Tansy felt the spray on her face. "You're mad."

"I'm curious. There aren't many places left to explore, are there? It's too late to be choosy. They're selling burgers in Antarctica."

"Send me a postcard."

"Do you think your mum and dad might stay on here, Tansy?" he asked, running after her.

"Why would they? They both like Bristol. They've got jobs." She walked on without looking back.

"Maybe they'd like this place better. It might be safer, you know. If what Dominic says is true."

Tansy looked at him drily. "All places are the same – remember that?"

"You're right, I know it," Harper admitted with his usual placidity.

But in her mind she saw, sharp as acid, a figure falling headlong from the Tor's height to the sea. A thing that wheeled and turned as it fell, flopped limply on to the rocks and tumbled off into water. It came with the clarity of a memory – a recent memory that set her trembling, wondering who that lost one might be.

"Talk of the—" Harper murmured to himself. He was squinting into the distance, inland. "Tansy, isn't that your dad?"

Tansy turned round. "Where?"

"On that ridge, the one where the thrift's growing so thick. Oh, it's hard to tell in this light."

Tansy squinted. Harper was right: there *was* a walker on the ridge, above the banks pink with thrift. He was, perhaps, two hundred yards away. A woman led him, but the sun-dazzle from something she carried obscured her. She was a camera flash, a wand to hold lightning. Tansy could hear the sound of a pipe being played, listened to it for some seconds, and found that the music was inside her head. But her father?

Yes! Yes, it *was* him! His walk was unmistakable. She recognised the streaks of red stitched into his coat, the glint of the sun on his bald crown (his monk's tonsure, Hilary had always called it). But who were those others following him? What was that grey, unreflective group that seemed to be always in shade, always casting their own shade on him? Walkers of course – but they lacked the usual hats and backpacks of the island's passing trade. They seemed forlorn, and they were leaking shadow. A cloud passed over and the group was lost as they headed into a gulley.

"Tansy, what's the matter?" Harper asked some seconds later. "Are you crying?"

"It's all right," sniffed Tansy. Tiresome boy with his unnecessary questions! But it wasn't all right and the tears would not stop.

"Here, Tansy, come here," said Harper. Her wet face was snuffling into the thin cotton of his shirt. It smelt of salt and sea and earth. His arm was round her. She could tell he was not looking at her, though, and she was grateful for it. She knew she would never love him that way. A gentle, self-sufficient light, that was Harper. But she had been wrong about so much and could not forgive herself. The Cursing Candle had not been responsible for Geoff's affair, she saw that now. But that did not mean there had been no curse. How could she have been so foolish as to think it? No, the magic would seek him out by different means, patiently, implacably. It would stalk him, and strike at last in a way she could neither guess at nor prevent. It would happen, soon. She had seen the fog of death upon him.

"I know what you're thinking," Harper said.

"You do?" Tansy blushed, in the privacy of Harper's shirt.

"I think so. You're wondering why it's always westward – am I right?"

"Uh?"

"Those walkers. Ever since we've been on Sweetholm I've seen them. Always in groups, always in the distance, always heading west towards the Tor."

Tansy wrenched her mind round to what he was saying. "That's where a lot of the cliff colonies are – kittiwakes and stuff," she suggested uneasily. "They're birdwatchers, probably."

"But you never see them coming back. They never come back to the Haven, do they?"

"Meaning what? What are you trying to say, Harper?"

"Can't you guess?" asked Harper. "Then I shouldn't have said anything." He removed his arm from Tansy's shoulder. She blinked at him stupidly, wondering what had happened. What was that expression forming on Harper's face? Then she had it.

"How dare you pity me!" she cried. "You clam up now and I'll spill your brains down this rock, I swear! What's going on?"

"I honestly don't know, Tansy! Don't be angry – I don't know what's happening. And my guesses are probably crazy. Why upset you with crazy things?"

"You *have* upset me, Harper. Get on with it."

Harper seemed not to know how to begin. At last he said, "I used to think this was all about Calypso. Now I'm not so sure. It was Dominic who got me wondering..."

Tansy waited. Suddenly, Harper asked, "What do you know about your Uncle John?"

"John? What's *he* got to do with anything?"

"Your uncle was going on a cruise, yes?"

Reluctantly, Tansy nodded.

"He was planning to, that's certain. My mum knew him quite well. Whenever she called round there'd be brochures and maps all over the place. He said the island was driving him mad. He couldn't wait to get away from Sweetholm."

"So where's the mystery? Are you saying he didn't make it?"

"All I know is, he'd been obsessed with those walkers for weeks before he disappeared. His precious guest rooms were standing empty, the ones he thought would make his fortune. Suddenly, the island was swarming with walkers, not just day trippers either. He couldn't work out where they were all staying. He started talking about another campsite, a secret one. He tried to follow them and came back bruised and swearing, worn ragged. I saw him once, about ten days before you and your parents got here. His eyes were wild. And Davy Jones says to him, 'You weren't close enough to see their faces, were you? Or to hear them if they called to you?' 'No,' says John. 'Why?' And Davy Jones looks very Welsh all of a sudden and says: 'Bad luck, very bad, to see their faces. To see your own face worst of all. That means a death.'"

"Davy Jones is a laugh riot."

Harper smiled a little – but what he said was, "No one knows more about Sweetholm than Davy."

15. The Lady's Finger

That morning, Geoff had set out on one of his philosophical rambles. He strolled among the flowering thrift in a daze of abstraction. He would imagine himself the master of the island, perhaps its only occupant. A benevolent Crusoe, he harboured a butterfly on his palm, coaxed the timid muntjac from its soil. It was easy to feel himself in harmony with nature – so long as he and nature were left alone.

More often, though, he thought about Tansy. So old, she seemed at times: but it was a child's face she had turned to him when he had told her about the affair with Gloria. Her story about a candle or potion or whatever had been nonsense, of course: but he shouldn't have let her see he thought so. He cursed himself, rubbing irritably at his forearm, which had begun to itch again. Magic had been last year's thing, a Kate Quilley thing. He had assumed that Tansy's interest would fade away, with the spots and the boy band posters. He saw now that he was wrong, and saw too that the anger she had been turning on herself all these months might very well now be directed his way. He must expect that and be patient under the lash of it.

A blue-black cap of cloud sat on the Tor, with a tasselled fringe overhanging the waters of the Channel. Boding it was now, and quiet. The sea was never more silent than at high tide, just the distant race of water running past the heel of Longholm. Later, the caves would be exposed and the sea-cut arches under Tower Rock. Then he would hear the artillery crash of waves tunnelling a way beneath his feet. *Rock of ages.* The childhood hymn sang in his ears, the triumphal organ with its bass pipe shaking body and soul together.

The master of Sweetholm felt as humble as an ant.

Geoff was roused by the sound of a scythe. It was Davy Jones, hacking at the edge of the alexander meadow. Though he was fifty yards further up the scree slope, the blade sounded alarmingly close: *scrrt, scrrt!* Davy kicked a stone down as he cleared the footslopes of the Tor and it came to rest at Geoff's feet. Davy had not seen Geoff, and Geoff watched his neighbour work: at first with amusement at his folly in trying to turn back nature's tide. The poor man really was a bit simple.

A little longer, however, and Geoff began to find something unsettling in Davy Jones's actions. In their strange fervour, perhaps. The red plumage of his Viking beard jerked from side to side, visible in odd flashes between the shrivelled heads of the alexanders. He grunted with the effort. An exotic creature, Geoff thought, of the foraging kind. A plunge, a swing with one hooked claw.

Or was it of the hunting kind?

Geoff passed on, beyond a blistered ridge of the Tor, and circled it to the limestone cliffs where the last of the cormorants and gulls still nested, the path known as the Lady's Finger. Bones crunched under his feet. Geoff was puzzled, until he remembered how the gulls were said to raid the takeaways five miles away in Plinth and cross the sea with their booty. Sweetholm had long been a resort of pirates. And these, no doubt, were chicken bones.

Another pebble came bouncing down from the Tor above

him. It ricocheted off the gravel path and fell into the sea. He glanced up, saw a gull flapping madly above. Its leg had been caught by something hidden among the rocks. The mewings of the bird were pitiable but Geoff could never have reached it: and besides, he feared its beak if he got too close. He walked a little faster, as the path around the Tor grew still more narrow and the cliff edge sidled closer. The way was beginning to seem perilous. Thirty yards of path were visible before the Tor elbowed it out of sight. The sun beat on the stones like a hammer and in the far distance he could hear Davy Jones working. *Scrrt, scrrt, scrrt.*

Then he felt his heart falter. There was a woman on the path ahead. A woman, where a moment before there had been no one. She was walking in the same direction as him. All he could see was the tall figure, the length of the hair that spilt over her shoulders, the boots, the jeans, the coat with the hood back. Well within calling distance, if Geoff had possessed the power of speech: but at that moment he was dumb. And besides, he did not wish to see that head turn, to see the face on it. Geoff's mind suddenly teemed with monstrous images, dredged from childhood. A death's head! A tusked gargoyle! A ravening lion! Worst nightmare of all, a featureless plain of drum-taut skin! He thought of them all, yet he was aware only that something impossible had happened and ought not to have. Was it – wasn't it – a person he knew? Wasn't it Gloria?

Though walking only slowly, the woman was already some distance away. If it was Gloria she must mean him to follow. He quickened his pace. She seemed to be walking at scarcely more than an amble, but to his surprise he did not gain on her. As the path grew temporarily wider, he even broke into a trot, but was immediately felled by a loop of creeper straggling down from the Tor. When he got up, winded, it was to see the top of the woman's body disappearing slowly below the level of the path.

Now at last he called her name, but she did not so much as

pause. The auburn head descended from sight.

Geoff arrived breathlessly at the place, ready to plunge down the slope after her. But there was no slope. Only the ending of the cliff and the sheer mortal drop of eighty feet to the sea. Geoff stumbled and fell again as he tried to check himself. He recovered with his head overhanging the crumbling turf. He looked around wildly. The grasshoppers whirred like clockwork. The sun beat. He heard his own hoarse breath gasping Gloria's name. He trembled at the thought of how close he had come to death.

But had that been Gloria, truly?

Here was a stone seat for travellers to sit on. It doubled as a weathered boundary stone, on which in 1860 a mason had chipped out the edge of the Bristol diocese, and the edge of the unhallowed Atlantic. Geoff slumped on to it. He no longer felt like Robinson Crusoe, not at all.

"Good morning, Mr Robinson."

Geoff looked up. Ten minutes had passed. Davy Jones was standing before him in a small pool of shadow. He wore a cap, and a straw-coloured budget was slung over his shoulder. "You look as if you have the cares of the world on your shoulders."

"I don't feel well," admitted Geoff.

"You shouldn't sit here in the sun then. Give me your hand."

Geoff held out his hand and Davy Jones pulled him to his feet. "That's a nasty burn you've got, Mr Robinson."

Geoff looked at his hand. The skin was flaking over, gleaming with scar tissue. "It's a rash. I must be allergic to something here."

"It looks like a burn to me. You should get it seen to."

"I should." Spotting a shaded part of the cliff walk Geoff added, "I think I'll just sit here for a few minutes, till the worst of the heat's over."

"You do that, Mr Robinson."

When Geoff looked up again he wasn't sure if he had slept.

Davy Jones was still standing nearby, but he was gazing at a point a little above Geoff's left shoulder.

"It's odd you should find yourself just here," said Davy, carrying on the conversation as if there had been no pause.

"Why so?" asked Geoff. Already he was feeling slightly put upon. He wanted nothing more than to stretch himself out on the flat stone and sleep.

"Only I remember you saying you were interested in the history of the island. Caves and the like."

"I think I did," Geoff yawned.

Davy Jones waited a moment. Then he asked in a quite different tone, "Do you call yourself a religious man, Mr Robinson?"

Geoff chose his words with care. "Not religious, but I hope a spiritual one. Why do you ask?"

"I am a religious man," said Davy Jones simply. "What do you know about the medieval priory?"

Geoff searched his mind for the correct reference. "Benedictine, wasn't it? St Brigan of Sweetholm. A local saint, I think."

"St Brigan, yes. The priory was dedicated to her. And before that the Celtic saints had built her a chapel, up on the Tor."

"I'd read that, of course," said Geoff, finding his feet again.

"Not one stone is left on top of another. But even before those early saints – even before Christ – Brigan had her worshippers. Then she was a goddess. Brigan was the herder of the dead and her home was this rough channel around Sweetholm. Below that first Christian chapel is another, one that survives."

"Really? A pre-Christian chapel? Well, I had no idea."

"No one does. Last summer I was combing the scree for useful stones, when I came across one that had been shaped by more than wind and weather." Davy Jones delved into his pocket and drew out a fist of rock. "You can see where the thing has been chiselled. And when I turned it over—"

"My goodness!"

"Yes? You know what you are looking at?"

"It's… is it an eye?"

Davy Jones nodded. "St Brigan watches over us, Mr Robinson. She never leaves me now."

"This really ought to be in a museum."

"I dug, but found no more such stones on the Tor. Instead, I nearly broke my neck with falling down an opening in the rock. And when I looked again at the stone I was sitting on, I saw that behind it was an entrance a man might just crawl through. That was Brigan's chapel."

He put the stone carefully back into his jacket pocket. Geoff looked up from it to find Davy Jones's own blue eye shot with flint.

"You wish to see the place?"

"I would love to," Geoff stammered, unnerved a little by the sudden proximity of Davy Jones's face. "At some future date. As you say, I have an interest in such things."

"That's why I'm asking you. I need your advice – as an educated man."

"But just now I think I should be getting back. I'm still not quite myself."

"Tomorrow afternoon then. Give me time to shut up the shop, though. How would 4.30 suit you?"

"Yes – yes, that would be splendid," said Geoff. "Tomorrow afternoon." He tried to sound clear-headed, but in truth his mind was still muzzy from the sun and it was all he could do to answer.

"Beside this bench then."

"Yes."

"Don't be late. Oh, and Mr Robinson?"

"Yes?"

"Keep it to yourself, will you? I don't want this cave to become a tourist attraction."

Geoff nodded. "I won't tell a living soul."

"I'll hold you to that," smiled Davy Jones.

16. Finding the Lady

"Do you know what this card is called, Calypso?" Gerard Winstanley asked. He held it up for her to see, but just out of reach.

"It's a Queen. The Queen of Clubs."

"Very good. Now, you can see where I'm putting the Queen, can't you?" Winstanley slipped the card into his breast pocket with an elaborate gesture. Calypso watched, dumb. "Do you think you can remember?"

Calypso nodded. "It's in your pocket."

"But now see." Winstanley picked up Calypso's wide-brimmed hat to reveal the Queen of Clubs again, lying face up on the table. He glanced up quickly, to check her reaction. But Calypso seemed still to be waiting.

"Are you going to put that one in your pocket too, Mr Winstanley?"

"Give it up, Gerard. She won't take your bait," said Sal, descending the stairs.

"Pardon me?"

"Trying to dazzle Calypso with sleight of hand. You're rusty. Your fingers are growing old."

"It's her *lack* of dazzlement that intrigues me. Nothing I do seems to surprise her. Calypso, do you think you can find another card like this?"

Calypso considered. She was willing to please Mr Winstanley, but his demands puzzled her. "I think there's one in Sal's belt," she said finally, eyeing the twisted string of beads Sal wore through the loops of her trousers. Sal looked down and found her hand closing upon a card – the Queen of Clubs. The bead string was threaded through its centre.

"These games are getting too much," Sal said. She looked at Calypso. "Well, Calypso? Why are you staring at me? Are you reading my fortune?"

Calypso shook herself out of what had seemed like a trance. "No, nothing. I didn't see anything."

"Because if there's something bad coming I don't want to know, OK? Gerard, you shouldn't encourage her."

"Forgive me, but I'm trying to discover just what the extent of her power is. Only then can we help her to control it. Calypso could be a tremendous power for good in the world, you know."

"Sophie brought her here because you promised a safe haven. She's not a laboratory rat."

"Have we finished?" Calypso fidgeted.

Winstanley sounded a warning note. "Now you're being mischievous, Sal."

"No – you're the mischievous one."

Sal's tone made Winstanley look at her curiously.

"What are you driving at?"

"My dad was a gambling man too. Oh, he wasn't good at it, not like you – but I learned to recognise that look in his eye."

"Now hang on, Sal—"

"You invest in things called Futures, right? But what if you had a little girl who could tell you what the future was going to be? A girl who could maybe make it happen, even? A man like you couldn't fail to see the possibilities…"

Gerard Winstanley looked angry. He could not speak – he *would* not, until he was sure his voice would obey him.

"You misjudge me, Sal. You know how I use my money – for the good of everyone."

"Perhaps," said Sal. "We'll see. I heard the Cronos takeover fell through. That must have left you seriously out of pocket."

"Have you been listening to Mike, Sal? Because I have to tell you I find that young man's continual cynicism little short of poisonous."

"I don't need Mike's help to see what drives you. You like to win."

Winstanley shook his head. "But not at the expense of others."

Sal gave him a thin smile. "So long as you understand me. Calypso is not to be exploited, Gerard. Sophie won't allow it and neither will I."

Winstanley snorted. "Before you accuse me of exploitation, think of your own behaviour. Think of what you've all had out of me the last two years."

"What we've had out of *you*! Oh, I could tell a story about that."

"Don't!" screamed Calypso. "Don't shout at each other!"

Sal stared. Winstanley opened his mouth to reply, but no sound came out.

"Bridget is angry with you both!" Calypso cried. "And you're both going to be sorry!" And snatching up her doll, she left the Manor House in tears.

★ ★ ★

Calypso lay amid the heather. Bridget was in her hand. She felt cold, until she saw the blue-tailed dragonfly hovering overhead and the spider with its hammock of web hoist between two grasses. Then she lifted her head, only to find that her long hair had caught itself on a stem of rosemary. She twitched herself free, carrying several spears of leaf with her.

Standing, she looked around. Nothing was familiar. On all sides the ground climbed gently, so that she stood at the bottom of a shallow dish. Alexanders and cow parsley surrounded her, the tallest plants outgrowing her easily. She clutched Bridget fiercely by the arm and tried to remember how she had come to be in this place. Mr Winstanley and Sal had been shouting, that was certain. The shouting had been bad, but worse was the anger that had discoloured Mr Winstanley's voice and hung like spent air after thunder. Then she could not breathe and had fled the place, with tears of frustration at her own clumsiness as she waddled and skipped through the yard and over the moat. But beyond that she remembered nothing.

Some animals – sheep, probably – had beaten out a path between the elder and crab apple trees. Barefoot, Calypso followed it up and out of the dish of ground. The turf was clenched and dry, and sprang back on her skin. Grasshoppers sang in the craggy gorse to either side. She shuffled between the bushes and the alexanders that overleant them, climbing always.

At the top of the dish was a sharp ridge. She had not been expecting it, an edge of vertical stone walling in the soil so abruptly. While beyond it… Calypso peered over and gasped. There was nothing. No more land. A blank wall of air only, in which the gulls, terns and fulmars hung quivering like grey stars. Calypso looked down, clutching her fingers tight round Bridget. In the narrow gulley below, the waves were in torment. Longholm's easternmost tip swooped out of the sea thirty yards away. There was a chaos of shattered limestone that broke each wave as it lunged across the narrow channel. Calypso licked salt from her fingers. Now, at low tide, the remains of a sea-hollowed arch could be seen. The arch had once bridged the gap between Longholm and Sweetholm, but ten thousand seas had breached it and it had fallen.

There were heads floating in the water. Longholm seals, fishing where the channel was narrow, had paused to look up at her. They were curious perhaps at the sight of a calico doll falling headlong down the cliff. For Calypso had now lost her footing and let her Bridget go. "Bridget!" she screamed.

But she did not see Bridget fall into the waves. When she dared peer over the rock to look directly, she found that Bridget had pitched on to a shelf of rock, not very far below. The shelf jutted out a yard from the cliff face and was thick with guano and the ever-present chicken bones. Bridget was splayed face up among it all and her smile was as wide and her cheeks as flushed as ever.

A jolt of pity and alarm shook Calypso: surely Bridget had not realised the danger she was in. A breath of wind might be enough to tilt her back over the cliff into the cauldron of sound and water below. Calypso considered briefly whether she might not climb down to rescue her. It was impossible. But to leave her there: oh, Bridget would be drowned! She thought with horror of Bridget's body sinking through the water, of the seals' muzzles tossing her high over the rocks, of the cruel limestone. She forgot that Bridget was only a doll, with a calico dress and painted eyes. There was no choice.

Without pausing she began to ease her legs over the cliff edge, holding a clump of grass to let herself down lightly. Her feet dangled free and she felt the salt mist as a new wave exploded in the channel below. Looking down, Bridget was visible as a patch of colour against the ferment. Rock, air and the whiskered heads of the seals spinning. The next moment Calypso had lost all sense of where she was and was afraid of falling skywards, to the small clouds marooned there. And her fingers had loosed themselves and she was flying.

17. St Brigan

Calypso *was* glad. Her doll was safe in the crook of her arm and her tangled hair was in a fair way to being straightened. The ledge, which could not have been as far down as she had thought, was behind her. What lay in front was no bare wall of rock, but an opening into the cliff. Inside she could see light: not one but many points of candle flame, half of them hanging in the air, the rest seeping out on the rock below or reflected starrily from pools of low water.

From across these pools of water came a whistle.

"Calypso! Over here!"

Calypso saw a man gesturing at her to follow him. Because of the way the roof dipped he was having to crouch, which made him look curious and not quite like a man at all. But Calypso recognised Davy Jones's voice.

"Calypso! Here, follow me!"

Calypso followed, her bare feet slopping through the broad puddles. She felt under her toe the collapse of plants, of tiny skeletons of shell or bone. There was a thickness to the water. The webbing of her toes dragged through with a slight reluctance and a coating of dark liquid clung to her shins and ankles. Most of all, though, she felt the constant breeze blowing seaward through the cave. It was the moor wind, lost and mournful in the dark, still carrying a sprig of lavender.

Davy Jones held his hand out and grasped Calypso's. She shrieked a little at his touch, for in this cold world Davy Jones's hand was trembling with excitement and was warmth itself.

"Thank goodness you are safe," he said avidly. "I knew you'd come."

"Will you take me home, Mr Jones?"

"Take you home?" Davy Jones seemed not to understand. Then he replied, "Yes, I'll take you home! Back to your own home, Calypso." And he gave her one of his jolly winks that did not look jolly at all by candlelight. He was not looking at her properly, Calypso thought. His eyes ranged over her, but did not meet her own. She shivered. "I'm cold here. Can we go now?"

They passed out of that cave and into another, at the narrowest point of which a rope dangled to the height of Calypso's head from a hole in the roof. But Davy Jones hastened her past to a third chamber. More fat church candles clustered on the clefts like rows of bats, and the cave wall was thick with wax. The smell of lavender was clogged now with another, heavier and more sickly: that of partly-digested meat. Calypso felt as if she had just walked into the belly of an animal.

"Mr Jones, where are we?" Calypso asked. She was not familiar with fear, but now she began to feel frightened, for she had just noticed that she and Davy were not alone. There was Someone in the chamber with them.

She folded Bridget into her chest and squeezed tight.

"The chapel," said Davy Jones.

He lit some of the candles that had faltered. A row lay at the feet of the Someone and by their rekindled light Calypso saw what kind of being it was who brooded here. It was a female figure, larger by far than any human being.

Mother! Calypso thought instinctively, though this was

nothing like Sophie and she felt no kinship with it. But a mother it was, a mother great and sorrowful. Davy Jones had set her head down over empty, cradled arms, so that her face was all but lost. Still, Calypso could see the orange blush of a crab shell and the dark eyes of mussel through the fronds that were her hair, and below them a wooden mouth's dark O was caught in lullaby. The note of the sea, gravelled under measureless tons of Sweetholm rock, sang from that mouth. The candlesmoke was bitter.

"St Brigan," said Davy Jones and he lowered his head at the name. Then, squatting beside Calypso, he added, "You have met her in your dreams, Calypso. Brigan of the Waves!"

"Is she alive?" asked Calypso. She wasn't sure of that at all.

"More so than you or me. Everything that breathes on this island is part of her life. She *is* Sweetholm."

Brigan's fingers were made of rough-carved wood. Calypso could not imagine that they had ever been touched with life. Yet Davy (or someone) had managed to slide a golden ring on to the fingers of her clenched left hand. How had he persuaded her to open out that palm? Calypso glanced quickly back to Brigan's face. It was smug with knowledge. She had the feeling that those eyes of mussel had just turned from her, that the wooden mouth's fixed O had flattened briefly, had smiled.

"How much have they told you, I wonder?" Davy Jones said. "Perhaps you never even asked. A child without both parents – that's hardly a matter for comment now. What do they tell you about your daddy?"

"I don't have a daddy," said Calypso simply.

"Do they say he went away?"

"If I did have a daddy, I don't think he would like you keeping me down here. Are you going to take me home, Mr Jones?"

"Calypso, of course I am!"

He took her on a path that led from Brigan, trailing off from the candlelight. At first Davy Jones led the way, chatting all the time as if they were on a ramble: stories of his own childhood, of Sweetholm in the days before tarmac. Calypso relaxed and laughed at his jokes though she did not understand them. She laughed and coughed up candlesmoke. Then they made a small twist and Calypso found that somehow she had overhauled her guide.

"Mr Jones?" she called in sudden fright, turning back.

However, she was alone. The cave seemed to have swallowed Davy Jones whole. It was very cold now. Only a narrow fissure in the rock before her gave a faint promise of daylight. Calypso put her head through: it was hardly wide enough for her to pass. A second fissure, narrower even than the first, flickered at the far end of this new cave. Between her and it lay a smooth and glassy darkness. She tried her weight upon the sloping ground. As she took her first step the ground suddenly dragged away and pulled her down to a ledge that overhung water. She screamed. She heard her own scream over and over again as the cave returned it. Then there was silence. This silence Calypso found oddly comforting: she felt as if she had become a part of the cave herself.

Calypso's wide eyes were keen in the dark, but at first she could see little, except that she stood on the shore of an underground pool, with rocks jutting from it. Then she realised that some of the rocks were moving. Something slid with reptilian ease into the water. A moment later the soft wake kissed her feet. She saw eyes that were discs of gun metal, of polished glass. And she heard the whisper of the water as the creature broke surface just before her.

Calypso stepped back, stumbling on the gravel slope. The face peering into hers was like nothing she had ever seen, and for all her picking at the future she had never dreamed of it. The eyes, to begin with, were not quite perfect in their inhuman roundness. There was a tweak of skin at their edges. The ghost of an iris, a pinprick pupil floated on their surface. No nose, but two guttered flaps of flesh that shrank and swelled. Elsewhere, the skin had hardened and cracked and become a supple armour of intersliding scales. In a sad mimicry of Brigan's sigh, the mouth sat with lips pouched almost too thick for speech.

Nevertheless, the thing spoke.

"My daughter," it said.

The first of four broad feet was splayed on the rock where Calypso crouched. Gradually the creature's long bulk was heaved forth, in a shadowy glimmer of scales. She could taste the hopelessness of its speech.

"Calypso," it said again. "My lucky charm…"

But Calypso did not answer, for she had fled in terror to the fissure and the hope of daylight.

18. Calypso and the Healer

"I found her on the moor," said Davy Jones. He took the thin body and rolled it on to a low divan. Calypso's fingers were brittle with cold. Davy Jones had wrapped her in his own coat, from which she stared back and flapped like a landed fish.

Sophie flew to her. "Calypso, Calypso! What's happened?"

Calypso's mouth opened and closed.

Sophie hugged her till her own knuckles whitened with the effort of holding her so close. "She's cold as earth!"

"I can't get a word out of her," said Davy Jones to the company now gathered in the dining hall of the Manor. Tansy stood with Sal and Harper. Mike was tense behind them, his mug of tea unregarded on the stone fireplace. Even Winstanley had been fetched down by the noise. And Calypso flapped, and her sound was not the sound of a child.

Dominic leant over her. He laid his fingertips on Calypso's face. Though his skin barely touched hers, it drew forth a stain that glowed on her cheek in a parody of health. They could hear the hiss of her breath.

"Stop it," Sophie pleaded, "you're hurting her." But Sal took her hand and whispered something, and Sophie held back as Dominic leant over her daughter again. By this time Calypso was coughing up water as though she had been dragged from the beach and not some upland slope. Her fingers, so white between Dominic's tanned hands, clawed his flesh. Dominic murmured words to himself, the same words that had brought healing to the sufferers in the camp at Lasithi. Under his hands he had felt leprous flesh become whole, seen lesions seal themselves, cleansed the malarial blood. Always it left him exhausted – and strangely humiliated too. For in this he was just an instrument, on which some force outside himself played. And that was no longer what he wished for, even if the player was God.

When he fell back, the colour had left his own cheek. It was obvious that something was wrong.

"The healing went straight through her," Dominic managed to whisper at last. His voice was hoarse. "As if she wasn't there! As if she was just a hole in the universe."

Sophie helped him to his feet and Winstanley came forward with a shot glass. "Here, drink this," he said. "It will help."

"I've never felt that before," said Dominic, ignoring him. "All the healing drained from me – gone! Not by Calypso, by something far beyond her…" He looked at his sister in bewilderment.

Sophie stood beside him. The smell of the sea was new and unmistakable. It came from Calypso.

"What's happening to her, Dominic?" Sophie demanded. "Don't you dare lie to me."

"Calypso has touched something that shouldn't even be in this world. Something evil. And what it finds, it *devours*."

Sophie gulped out an exclamation and broke down. Mike knelt beside her. "Don't listen to that voodoo talk. I've heard these shamans ranting. When they haven't got an answer they blame the gods."

"You don't understand," sobbed Sophie, "he's telling the truth. I smelt this once before."

The room was silent. Everyone looked at Sophie. "Tell us," urged Dominic. "If you want to help Calypso, tell us everything now."

"You already know. Joe was out night-swimming and the incense was spitting in the fire, and I was too stupid to realise what it was that was making us all behave that way…"

Sal took her in her arms and looked back at Dominic resentfully. "It wasn't for this I brought you to Sweetholm!"

"It's better that you did," he muttered.

Tansy was at the open window, where the blue sky overhung their roof like a cracked dish. The Manor's moat and its turf banks held back an encroachment of unruly alexanders, spiked dragon heads of thistle. A photograph of this would show nothing but a perfection of light. A recording would reveal only the wheedling complaint of the gulls, slung out on the sea's distance. Sweetholm was a seductive place. Easy to see what drew people to it, what made them stay. Not the beauty alone, but the separateness, the feeling that in this living ark one might be saved, whatever calamity overwhelmed the world. That must be what the ancient monks had felt, snug in their cloister while Europe became a charnel house. On Sweetholm, at least, they would be safe. They little thought what slid through the grass of their Eden. But Dominic knew.

"It's the island!" he said. "Calypso must leave Sweetholm at once. Mr Winstanley, how soon can we move her?"

"Move her? Are you serious?"

"Dominic, you don't understand," said Sophie. "This place has been her nursery. She's been happy here. Until she came she didn't even speak, did you know that? Not a word, except to me. Anyone official and she closed up like a fist. And you want her to go to hospital?"

"I didn't say hospital," responded Dominic. "But she must leave Sweetholm, now."

Sophie blinked back at him. The idea seemed virtually incomprehensible.

"Haven't you suspected?" he said. "I could feel it even as I came over in the ferry, though there was too much distraction then – I didn't understand it." He took Calypso's hand again. "Sweetholm is one of the frayed places of the world. I have been in others and I know the signs. In Lasithi, when the Red Leprosy first broke out, it was the same. There was always more to it than illness. At night the sky was dark with flocks of birds. There was a well in the town where the people wouldn't draw water because of the voices they heard. I saw the names of the old gods scratched on the roof."

"What has any of this to do with Calypso?" demanded Winstanley in exasperation.

"You're right," Dominic acknowledged, raising his hand. "Such stories are endless. But together they point only one way – to a breach between this world and its shadow. Sophie, you know very well why Calypso could be the perfect bridge from the demon-world to this. From the moment of her conception she has worn enchantment like a stain. But now she has met something that knows how to take her power for its own ends, to shape and use it."

Several eyes turned to Sophie. She had listened to her brother without expression. "No one's taking Calypso anywhere," she said.

"Somewhere on this island a demon is hauling itself out of limbo. It is making itself real again. It has found devotees already, perhaps – it will be hungry for worship. It will establish a sanctum, a holy ground. And it will require sacrifice—"

"We don't have to listen to this," said Mike. "You love it, don't you, priest? Ghosties and ghoulies!"

"If you discover this sanctum you must not hesitate – destroy it," Dominic continued obliviously. "That's the only way.

Meanwhile, take Calypso from the island while you still can. Please!"

In the silence that followed, Tansy looked around the room. Sophie did not seem to be listening to her brother's words at all, but was whispering into Calypso's ear, songs and favourite rhymes that might lure her back. Mike was mute with indignation. Harper, like most of the rest of them, seemed to be waiting for Gerard Winstanley to speak.

"I don't think Sophie should be rushed into anything," Winstanley began. "No doubt you believe what you say, but this must be her decision. You owe her that."

"Then there's no hope," said Dominic.

Sal prepared a poultice to draw out the cold phlegmatic humours that had robbed Calypso's body of life. They laid her, first of all, on half a dozen blankets before the fire, where the pale light flickered on her skin. All afternoon she spent in half slumber, in undirected sighs. Nor would she finally settle until Sophie had carried her to her own bed in the cot room above the dining hall. And there her dreams were troublesome.

19. Mr Robinson Underground

Geoff walked with a stave now, one that he had found beside the road to the Haven. It was polished and comfortable in his hand, with a bulging knot to stop his fist slipping as he levered himself over the walls and ditches. Gone was the oppressive heat of the previous day, which had so fuddled his brain. He saw now that his vision of Gloria had been no more, perhaps, than a mild case of sunstroke. Foolish to read more into it.

He had still been rather groggy when he had returned to Crusoe's Castle that night. Tansy had treated him like an invalid, an attentiveness for which he had been grateful at first; but the sense of being under her eye had grown ever more oppressive. As for Hilary, she hardly spoke to him these days, unless to administer some barb or other. He had begun to treasure the thought of this secret expedition. It would be an adventure, the kind he had read about as a boy. So now he was making for the place where he had almost fallen, the stretch of cliff called the Lady's Finger, there to meet Davy Jones.

Halfway to the Tor Geoff stopped, and sat upon a wayside stone. He was not tired yet, but as he made a fuss of tightening his shoelace he cast frequent glances, both to the Tor ahead and back down the road he had just travelled. In the far distance he could just make out the whitewashed walls of John's Folly.

"No need to worry," he told himself. "Tansy's out and Hilary will still be sorting through that catalogue Davy brought round. She never walks as far as the Tor. Besides, I've nothing to feel guilty about." He added this last comment out loud and in a rather belligerent tone.

Of course, he was absolutely alone and he had no reason to feel guilt. But he could not quite rid his mind of the notion that someone was following him over the lonely moor road. He started. What was that shadow gliding swiftly across the open ground to his left?

No more than a cloud's shadow, no more than that.

Ashamed, Geoff got to his feet and, stave in hand, set his face firmly towards the Tor. He felt himself hurrying to his appointment. A breeze snaked through the alexander meadow. Distantly, he could see a pair of walkers, perhaps half a mile away. Above his head, the sobbing of the gulls was frayed by wind and sea.

Inexorably, Geoff found himself being consumed by a sense of horror. Not of being seen, he realised, or even of Davy Jones. It was horror of the island itself, of Sweetholm — how ridiculous! But he walked on like a man under a doom. His expedition west had assumed in his mind the force of a destiny and it was a clockwork man who walked and clambered the last mile, who saw how many more of those scuttling shadows chased past him to settle about the Tor's skirts.

He began now, as the sun reached its height, to negotiate the final stage of his journey. A gull swooped down, a bumble bee swung near and far about his head. Geoff noticed these things, but did not heed them. He was some fifty yards short of the bench when he heard a whistle from above and there was Davy himself. Davy stood at the upper end of a steep gulley drifting with loose stones. A rope was looped diagonally from shoulder to waist and his scythe was propped beside him.

"You took me by surprise," said Geoff, feeling foolish for having been startled.

Davy nodded and tossed Geoff a loop of rope. "Up here. It's quicker than the path."

Geoff wound the rope about his fist and fought his way up the gulley, to be clapped on the back by Davy Jones as he made the top of the ridge. Davy smelt of clay and smoke, and at his back a crooked battalion of weeds sloped arms. Davy snapped their stems under his foot as he led Geoff up higher, then beyond an outcrop which ran down to a cup of grass and low bushes.

The cave mouth was hidden. Sweetholm was said to be riddled with caves, but the entrances were lost, to the sea or some tattered legend of ghosts and elf-shot. Geoff remembered seeing such stories in the pamphlets of Sweetholm anecdotes sold to tourists in the Haven. Davy Jones lifted a hedge of brambles carefully aside. Within there was blackness.

"The slope inside's too steep to climb down," said Davy Jones. "Here's where the rope earns its keep." He took the coil of rope he carried and tied it to a nearby trunk, then spooled it in. "It's all right," he said, noticing Geoff's nervousness. "I'll go first."

Davy Jones disappeared into the cave. A few seconds later, Geoff heard himself being bidden to follow. Geoff tugged nervously at the rope, reassuring himself that Davy's knot was fast. "Can you manage, Mr Robinson?" called Davy Jones's voice from below. The hint of mockery in it was unmistakable.

Geoff let himself down, fist by fist. With remarkable speed the daylight was lost and a pool of cold air began to overwhelm him. There was no sound but his own laboured breathing and the impatience of Davy Jones below.

"Come on, man, you're almost there now. It's only a few feet down!"

At last, Geoff's feet touched solid ground. He let go of the rope and, though it was virtually dark, dusted himself off. Davy Jones lit a flashlight.

"So where is this Brigan?" asked Geoff, trying to sound as if he descended into underground chapels daily. In truth, he was beginning to perspire, despite the chill of the cave. He found himself reflecting that he should have thought to tell someone where he was going. A mumbled message to Hilary about exploring the western end of the island would not do. Accidents happened to people in places like this. Non-accidents too. And no, he didn't trust Davy Jones one bit.

"Look up!" said Davy. "The saint is smiling at you!"

Geoff raised his eyes to the roof of the cave, where Davy Jones's flashlight had put darkness to flight. Geoff did not see the face immediately. The angle was wrong and under the flashlight's play the very surface of the rock seemed to shift – or to have just shifted. He could not get it out of his head that something was clinging to the roof above him.

The flashlight gave the rock an outline of sharp shadow; but its movement in Davy Jones's hand gave the shadow movement, transformed it to hands or feet, or to a mass of furled drapery. A long, pained face was suggested and the hollow of a mouth. Two eyes, also black and hollow. Yes, he could see how the shadow gave a twitch to corners of those eyes and how the lips formed – not a smile exactly, for nothing could make this other than a sorrowful face – but an expression at least of welcome, perhaps blessing. But this was not the end of his pilgrimage, not just yet. Davy took his hand – his own were warm with excitement – and led him down further.

"This is where the monks came," said Davy Jones, "when the Black Death reached Sweetholm. First for refuge and then to die." Here they had to bow their heads, for they were passing under a low arch. The rock beneath their feet had acquired a thin film of water. "They fell sick with the fever. Pustules broke from their skin and turned those holy men to stinking corruption. The little graveyard was full in less than a week."

"I see," Geoff murmured, wondering why Davy Jones was telling him all this.

"In their panic, they began to throw the bodies into the sea. Three anchorites were living on Longholm: the monks would use ropes to lower food from the cliff above. But the anchorites cut the ropes. They preferred starvation to the death they might suffer from the plague. Soon, no one was left to send them food in any case. The priory garden was left to gulls and crows."

Geoff opened his mouth to remark that this story, if true, could not be known to Davy Jones, since he had allowed for no survivors. But almost at once they arrived at their destination, the small, pot-bellied chamber in which Brigan brooded. Davy Jones said, "I think it was here they came, to St Brigan, their patroness. Here their bodies lay: and when she wept, her tears floated them out towards Longholm, her own island. There, so one story says, she turned them into seals. And there they remain her liegemen."

The candles that ringed Brigan were all extinguished, but for a few embers of tallow which brightened with the breeze of their approach. Geoff's impression was that their path had been a downward one, and that they now stood nearer the centre of the Tor. Certainly the level of the water here was deeper, though by what combination of natural forces he had come to be standing in six inches of water he could only guess. Rain seepage, capillary action, the sheer upward pressure of the tide upon the unguessed underwater caves − all might have contributed to the discomfort he now felt between his toes. Above that level, he laid the blame squarely on Davy Jones.

Davy Jones's flashlight swept to the only significant object in the cave, Brigan herself. Beyond a slight intake of breath, he said nothing. Apparently, he wished to leave comment to Geoff himself. Geoff, meanwhile, was thinking fast.

"Is this your work?" he asked. The shrine before him was obviously of recent date. Was it perhaps meant as a work of art? "Did you create this… phenomenon?" He let the question hang, ready to leap either way.

"I found her holy spring and restored her shrine," Davy Jones replied. "But creation is never a one-way affair, Mr Robinson."

"Well," Geoff answered with a laugh, "I hope you don't think this little goddess was responsible for creating *you?*"

Davy Jones stepped back, as though Geoff's remark had shocked him. "I have been no more than a tool fit for her hand. Through me she has gained a little life and a few offerings that have pleased her."

"Offerings?"

Davy lowered his head. "My love and service," he said, speaking softly. "The blood of your brother, John, to consecrate this chapel. A priestess to show Brigan's power and honour to the world."

Geoff tried to laugh, but the back of his throat had gone suddenly dry. "John? My brother? Are you saying he's dead?"

"He passed into the service of the goddess," said Davy Jones piously. "As you must too, Mr Robinson."

"Now hang on a minute," said Geoff. "My life's already spoken for. I'm using it myself."

Davy Jones laughed a little. "The mark on your arm shows you to be dedicated. Didn't you know you had a brand? Didn't you taste the wormwood in your mouth?"

"It's just a rash, Davy, I told you." Geoff tried to sound calm. "I think we'd better leave now."

Davy Jones did not reply. The torch clicked off.

Several seconds passed.

"Davy? What happened? Did you drop the torch?"

Geoff knew that Davy Jones had not dropped the torch. There had been no clatter of plastic upon stone. But anything was preferable to the silence in which he now found himself stranded. The taste of wormwood was already bitter on his tongue.

"Lost, Mr Robinson?" It was Davy Jones's voice, some distance away. "See if you can smell your way home."

Geoff tried to calm himself and began by taking several very deep breaths. Once his eyes got used to the dark, he found that he could see a little, thanks to the candle embers and the light from a narrow shaft in the rock nearby. There was no question of escape that way, unfortunately: it was much too strait a path. He returned, led partly by touch, to the place where they had entered the cave. The opening was still there above his head, but the rope had been withdrawn.

Geoff began to feel sick. However, there must be at least one more entrance, presumably at the western end of the cave, for when he flicked his lighter open he found his flame bent that way by the breeze. Besides, in a place like Sweetholm he would soon be missed and, once missed, found. Any search party would make its way to the Tor very quickly. Then it was simply a matter of shouting himself hoarse.

But outside Davy Jones had begun to sing in his sonorous baritone: a grand old hymn tune. Geoff could see his sunlit boots shuffling back and forth overhead, and the end of a long stick dragged after him.

"Davy? Let down the rope, for heaven's sake!"

The footsteps stopped. The singing stopped. Davy Jones seemed to be rummaging through his belongings at the entrance to the cave. Geoff assured himself that he was about to lower the rope after all.

Then he heard the sound of a blade being sharpened.

Geoff did not wait for more. He followed the breeze to the western end of the cave. It was not long before he discovered the outer chamber leading to the sea. The sound of the waves excited him, and the growing light, and he splashed towards it.

He found himself on a small ledge, with an unscalable overhang above his head. Beyond the edge of the cliff he saw the clouds flitting. It gave the illusion that he himself was moving. He became dizzy with the thought of it: the whole cliff face falling, and taking him down.

"Davy! Davy Jones!" he shouted. Then, thinking better of it, he cried out, "Anyone! Is there anyone there? Please help me!"

But there was no one. Besides, his shouting seemed to have disturbed the kittiwakes on the cliffs nearby and a raucous outcry drowned his calls.

Minutes passed, then hours. At first, he expected Davy Jones to follow him – either to lead him to safety with some kind of apology or else to carry through his attack. After a while he ceased to care which. As the sun fell over Longholm, Geoff sat looking west. He couldn't believe it. That a cave with three entrances should have, for him, no exit. Was it possible – really possible – that he would *die*?

He peered through the sea spray at Longholm, where the seals lived. There were several there right now: watching him. The heads of the seals were cowled, in aspect rather grave. He found himself remembering what Davy Jones had told him about those monks. Perhaps they really had been transformed by Brigan's magic! Perhaps they *were* her liegemen! He smiled a little at the thought, despite his gloom.

In reflections such as these, tossed between hope and fear, Geoff Robinson settled down to spend the short remainder of his day. He slept at last. And woke to a blinding moon, a sea lying vast and fallow. A sea-tuned music stole over his mind as he looked to the rocks below, to the dazzling figure who waited there. She was calling him. Brigan's voice was fretting the air, calling him by name, teasing out the twine of his bright soul and drawing it down, as docile as a cloud, across the broken channel towards Longholm.

20. Plagues on Both Houses

"Look!" whispered Tansy. "I saw her lips move."

Tansy, Harper and Sophie sat together. It was six in the morning and they were at the Manor, beside Calypso's bed.

"I didn't see anything," said Harper.

"You're half asleep still. Watch!"

"I think Tansy's right," said Sophie. "Something's changed."

Five hours they had sat without a sound from Calypso, whose sleep had plunged her deep into the well of her own mind and sealed her there. Sophie had been afraid that she would die, and the people of the Manor were taking it in turns to keep a vigil. The evening before, Tansy had phoned her mother.

"It's the little girl who lives here," she had told Hilary. "Calypso – she's in a bad way: I said I'd take a turn at watching her tonight."

"If you want," sighed Hilary without interest.

"You don't mind, do you? Harper's mum will talk to you about it, if you like."

"No, no, it's all right, Tansy. I'll see you in the morning, I suppose."

"Mum? Are you okay?" Tansy had been expecting at least a show of reluctance at the idea of her spending the night at Harper's house.

"I'm fine," said Hilary in the same listless tone.

"And Dad?" Tansy dared to ask. "Is he all right too?"

"Your father? Never better, I'd say."

Harper was at Tansy's elbow. "Can you stay?"

Tansy nodded, frowning, and replaced the receiver.

"Good – Calypso needs your company tonight, Tansy. She likes you, you know."

Calypso was certainly talking now. They craned forward to listen. Her lips quivered, and blew out words like bubbles. Her eyes flickered as Sophie opened the shutters, pale with the light on them.

"Hide me," said Calypso, fumblingly at first. But her eyes suddenly opened like trapdoors. "*She knows where I am!*"

"Shh, darling. You've had bad dreams, that's all."

"Don't let me go to sleep," Calypso pleaded, catching hold of Sophie's arm. Already the spasm was past and an undertow of sleep was dragging her back. "That's where she'll find me. She's not nice," Calypso whimpered, but her voice was thick and slurred. "Not nice at all…"

"Who's not nice?" Tansy whispered urgently. "Tell us, Calypso!"

But Calypso was no longer there to hear her.

★ ★ ★

When Tansy returned to Crusoe's Castle, she found her mother outside, sitting in a foldaway chair. She was facing the road. Tansy could tell by the set of her shoulders that something was wrong.

"Hello Mum," she began warily.

Hilary barely glanced at her. She could not raise the energy to reply.

"Mum, what's the matter?" asked Tansy.

"This time he's really done it," said Hilary with heavy finality.

"Who?" Tansy began – then stopped, seeing the red rims of her mother's eyes.

Hilary tossed her a crumpled piece of paper. Tansy found that she was holding a receipt for a ferry ticket. "What's this?"

"Isn't it obvious? Your father's done a bunk. Gloria Quilley's attractions have proved too much for him, it seems."

Tansy looked carefully at the receipt. It had yesterday's date and the name of the ferry on which they had sailed to Sweetholm. No passenger name.

"There's some mistake here. This isn't his."

"He didn't come home last night. He'll be long gone by now, with that kind of start. There's no mistake, Tansy. Only mine, and that was big enough." Hilary wiped her face with her sleeve.

"I don't understand," floundered Tansy. "When did you last talk to him?"

"Yesterday lunchtime. He said he and Davy were going to look at some old ruins up near the Tor. I should have seen through that one!"

A cold trickle of sweat ran down Tansy's back. "Him and Davy? And you've not seen him since?"

Hilary shook her head.

"But, Mum – have you thought that something may have happened to him? On the Tor, I mean?"

"It's hardly Everest, Tansy," said Hilary. "And you're forgetting the ferry ticket."

"Mum, this receipt could belong to anyone!"

"It was stuck down the side of the armchair, the one he reads in. He's always losing things there." Hilary turned to her for the first time. "It's no good, Tansy. I know you're trying to help, but I've given up pretending not to notice things. The phone calls with no one at the other end. It's a ticket for yesterday and no one else has sat in that chair since we arrived."

Was that true? Tansy couldn't remember. "I'll go down to the Haven," she said. "We can easily settle this. The harbour master will remember if Dad took the ferry."

Hilary considered a moment. "If you insist," she said, raising herself from the chair. She began to make her way to the car, then turned sharply and said in a voice that was oddly hostile, "But I'll go alone."

So Tansy was left to sit in the foldaway chair and clench her hands and wonder. If Dad was really gone, then everything was changed. The meaning of this summer, the island, their whole life there. Sweetholm no longer seemed quite real to her. Was it a place where people really lived and died? A home, possibly? No: it was just a leaky raft thrown out and left to drift, while Britain, a short gull's flight away, steamed on heedlessly. There was Geoff being hauled on board, clapped on the back, losing himself amid the mountainous decks, the pillars of chrome and marble, while the liner's wake curved back and all but sank them.

She felt the dull resentment creeping over her like a second skin, binding back her thoughts. As she sat in her mother's chair, she saw Geoff as her mother had seen him. Anything else seemed too much effort. The picture seeped through her mind, from imagination to thought to certainty: Geoff had left them, Geoff was gone. Every twittering bird sang of it. The island wanted her to forget, to ease Geoff from her thoughts and begin anew. Here. On Sweetholm.

When she heard the car crunching over the drive she ran out to meet her mother. "Well?" she cried as the engine cut out. "What do they say in the Haven? Has anyone seen Dad?"

Hilary climbed out, then stooped back to retrieve her bag. The weight that pressed her shoulders down was almost tangible.

"Did you talk to the harbour master?"

"His office was empty, Tansy. And the ticket office was closed. But I met Davy Jones coming out of his shop, and he said… Oh hell, Tansy, do I have to do this every time?" She fumbled a handkerchief from her pocket and sniffed loudly. "Half of it's the hay fever, you know."

"Yes, I know that can set you off," said Tansy and waited patiently.

At last her mother said, "Davy didn't know anything about this trip to the Tor. That was a fairy tale, just as I said. Geoff's gone all right."

"Without any bags packed?"

"You know him better than that. He always was impulsive and when it comes to packing he has no more sense than a newt."

"If you believe Davy Jones!" said Tansy bitterly.

Hilary looked at her oddly. "And why shouldn't I believe Davy? No, Tansy, we have to face it, we're stranded here." A strange half-smile touched her. "Marooned in paradise."

Tansy walked to the Haven herself. On the waterfront, gulls were circling. As usual, the place seemed half deserted, though the Inn exhaled a stale and sordid laughter as she passed. Through its frost windows moved the shapes of men and there was brass gleaming. When she turned away, it was to find a gull perched on the bollard behind her, cocking its head. No Geoff.

A few yards along the front was Davy Jones's shop, which was indeed shut – and bolted. Inside, she could see the cupboards and boxes painted in summer blue, marine green, just as Harper had described. Driftwood mirrors stared back at her from the far wall, and between her and them stood shell-encrusted caskets, handmade greetings cards crinkly with weed, sand pictures of murderous complexity. She saw clocks and ladles, and wooden automata who would chop wood or row a boat at the turn of a handle. A pair of marionettes was dangling from the ceiling near the window, inked with solemn little faces. One had its arms flung high, as if in surprise or surrender; the other was limp.

Bizarrely, Davy Jones had hung them by their necks, so that in the semi-darkness Tansy seemed for a moment to be witnessing an execution. In fact she now saw that the two puppets were not alone, that a congregation of them extended all the way to the back of the shop. And something about the impossible contortions of their limbs, the knots throttling those bloodless necks of wood, the sheer *number* of them, sickened her. The shop was a massacre. A forest. An inverted forest of hanging men.

As she turned away in sudden disgust she noticed that the sky was growing hazy. A fog was rising as the air cooled to evening. She could even see it brimming towards them from the farthest Channel, rolling with the power of a tidal bore between the northern and southern banks. As the light played over its surface, the fog changed shape, mouthing faces at her and scattering shadows like nervous birds. The sight disturbed her almost as much as the marionettes had done. She turned and climbed the steep moor road.

The ghost of her father walked with her. Each breath of wind seemed charged with his presence, his absence. They had lived on Sweetholm only a few weeks, but the memories shot at her like snipers' bullets, from every plant and rock. There was the very wall which had nearly taken the paint off the car's passenger door. This was the corner where he had offered Dominic a lift. And so on and on. It was inescapable. Now Hilary was convinced that he had left them. Hilary had Geoff's past to point to, of course. She had that ferry ticket too (but Davy Jones could easily have planted it, Tansy thought with a sudden insight). Except for a glimpse of distant colour on the moor two days ago, Hilary might be right. But Tansy did not believe it. Somehow her curse had tracked Geoff down. It had left him at the mercy of this dream-haunted island. He was somewhere on Sweetholm, in need of help or beyond help altogether. Either way it was up to her to find him.

It was mid-afternoon before Tansy returned. The house was empty, but in the garden Hilary was spraying roses. Tansy watched her from the kitchen door. Her mother was humming to herself, tuneless tunes under her breath. "They bloom such a short time," she said as she saw Tansy. The roses on John Robinson's trellis, a fine sight from the empty guest rooms, were not yet half over. Tansy said so.

"They know I care for them," said Hilary, giving the vermin a final souse.

"They're lovely flowers," Tansy offered tentatively.

"Aren't they just? My father used to say that garden flowers were a poor imitation of wild ones. But I say paradise was a garden, not a meadow. A garden. You know, Tansy, in a different world I might easily have been a horticulturalist. If I hadn't had this, this" – Hilary waved her hand about, trying to swat the right word from the air – "this dreadful sense of *duty*. Which is just another word for guilt really."

"Mum," said Tansy slowly. "Have you thought any more about Dad?"

Hilary gave a small start. "And what is there to say on that score?"

"He hasn't rung, has he? Because—"

"You're so naïve, Tansy," Hilary reproved her. "No, I think your father will be lying low for a long time. Till Gloria tires of him, I dare say."

Hilary picked up her rose-spray again and resumed her humming. Tansy waited till she could bear no more.

"Mum, you've got to stop this!"

"Stop what, darling?" said Hilary, a hideous brightness glossing her voice.

"That humming, for a start. Please, it's not fair."

"What isn't fair?"

"To leave me… *alone* like this."

It was a bad choice of words. Hilary looked her straight in the eye for the first time. "You haven't much to teach *me* about being left," she said tartly.

"See! You do mind! Why can't you come right out and admit it?"

Hilary stopped her spraying with some effort. "Of course I mind. But Geoff Robinson is not the be all and end all of my life – or yours. When I look around me I find myself in a beautiful place, doing work I can see is worthwhile, *growing* things…"

"Marooned, you called it."

"Marooned from what?" Hilary came over to her. "Look, I don't know exactly what you expect of me, but it sounds as if you want me to be punished twice: once for having a two-timing husband and again for losing him. But why? Why should I be punished? I'm not the one who walked out."

Tansy wanted to be courageous. She wanted to tell Hilary about seeing Geoff on the moor and about everything that had led to it, including the curse. "I don't want you to feel guilty," she began. "That's the last thing I want. If anything, it's me who should feel—"

"Feel what?" interrupted Hilary.

"Nothing. It's just – I'm lonely too!"

At that, Hilary smiled. She held her arms out and they hugged. "Come here, come here," said Hilary and kissed her on the forehead.

Tansy stood back from their embrace, about to speak. But already Hilary was taking off her gardening gloves and declaring that all this would never get dinner on the table. She began to pack away the insecticide.

Tansy watched in dismay. Her skin was still moist from the touch of her mother's lip. The echo of her words was in her ear. But the words had no meaning: they were a dismissal. Hilary wanted nothing from her that she could give, and could offer nothing. Tansy felt herself grow stiff and inflexible. Sweetholm was indeed a small island.

She said, "I'm going to the Manor again. I'll probably stay the night."

Hilary looked at her in surprise. "Why exactly?"

"The sick girl I told you about – Calypso. They're all very worried. I want to help out if I can."

"That boy will be there too, I suppose," said Hilary drily. "Prancer or Dasher or whatever his name is."

"Mum!"

Hilary hesitated, then waved her away. "Go then. If you think that's where you're needed most."

Tansy looked on in resentment as Hilary bent to pull a leek for supper. "I haven't any doubt of it," she said.

21. Dusk on Sweetholm

Walking westward, Tansy thought the Tor looked larger than before. Larger, darker and loomingly bleak, its face stubbled with black leaves and broken rock. It sneered down at the Manor buildings, scattered like toys at its feet. The slender moon winked and shivered, while on the moor road the sheep ran off skittishly as Tansy passed. Everywhere she found the same feeling of dread reflected back at her, the same crushing vulnerability. This feeling (she saw it now) had been growing since her arrival on Sweetholm. It had all been building to this moment – to this night. She could no longer see the landward fog, but she knew it was coming. It was pawing its blind way along the channel, drawn by smell and by its own vast hunger.

Of course it was coming. She had summoned it herself.

She crossed the moat into the Manor, but saw no one. Only Mike in the distance, putting some machinery under tarpaulin. He too had an intuition of bad weather, it seemed. Tansy went directly to Calypso's cot room. Calypso was still there, wrapped in her crocheted blanket. When Tansy entered, Harper looked up from the floor where he had been sitting cross-legged.

"Any change?" Tansy asked.

Harper's face was pale. He didn't need to answer.

Tansy took one of Calypso's hands, holding it close between her own. "Poor scrap."

"She's half-awake, most of the time," Harper said. "We hear her calling names. Sometimes, though, she's so quiet, I have to put my hand to her mouth to make sure she's still breathing."

"Where's Sophie?"

"Sal persuaded her to rest. She's been watching for two days now. She's exhausted."

"Has she said anything about taking Calypso off the island?" Tansy asked suddenly. "There's a fog rising."

"Dominic still wants her to. He's upstairs now, trying to get Winstanley on his side. But Sophie won't, I'm sure."

Tansy heard the despondency in his voice. "You believe him, don't you?" she said, folding down the blanket.

"What do you mean?"

"Dominic — you believe what he says. There is a power here working through Calypso. A god, a demon — whatever."

"I don't know," said Harper. "Everyone's behaving very strangely." He went to the window, where the shadow of the Tor had stolen almost to the Manor ditch. As his shoulders hunched, Tansy felt she could read his mind.

"You do — you know it. It's got Calypso and now my Dad has disappeared and my mother hardly bats an eyelid. I think Davy Jones is involved too. There's a spell on this island — and it comes from there," she said, pointing.

"What?" asked Harper, distracted. "Oh, yes. The Tor."

"Remember what you said about the walkers? Always going westward, always towards the Tor?" She broke off, then added, "The Tor *is* Sweetholm."

As soon as she said it, Tansy knew that it was true. From the Tor you could see thirty miles in any direction: the cathedral towers of four cities; the moon's path leading west; the liquid thickness of a galaxy overhead.

"I'm worried about Calypso," Harper said simply.

Tansy came to stand beside him. A recklessly simple thought occurred to her. It was an inspiration. "We could go tonight!" he said.

"Uh?" said Harper, not comprehending her.

"We could go to the Tor tonight – you and me. We could end this thing ourselves."

"*Us*? How?"

Tansy's eyes were bright. "Remember what Dominic said. This demon will need a foothold in the real world – a sanctum. If we can find that and destroy it—"

Harper stared at the glass. "It'll be dark soon," he said and there was a tincture of Hilary's heavy listlessness in his voice.

"*Dark?*" repeated Tansy scornfully. "You're scared of the dark?"

"I only meant—"

"And if the morning's too late?" she demanded. "We've wasted too much time already."

In the corner, Calypso clutched her doll closer to her heart and shuddered.

"What's holding you back, Harper?"

"I don't want to break my neck, that's all. You're mad, Tansy."

"I'm not mad. If there's nothing to find, why then we'll find nothing! But if there is…"

Harper stared at her, pulling at his fingers' ends. But Calypso was still stirring and this time her cries had brought Sophie in.

"If you don't come, I'm going on my own," said Tansy, daring him.

"You're mad," he repeated. "Stark and staring."

An hour later, Sophie was alone in the room, watching over her daughter. Calypso's slumbers were not easy. The silence of the house pressed in on her. The blue towel she loved was wrapped about her wrist and Bridget (known as Queenie) had slipped down and hung from the pillow now by the pinched cloth of her skirt. Calypso was walking a causeway between waking and sleep. She was looking for something she had left behind in Brigan's cave and could not find it. She had been looking for a long time, for centuries, and now from the misted distance a voice was calling her. It was Brigan's voice – not old and pale, but the voice of a true goddess, whose promise will be kept. Rest after toil, ease after pain, home after wandering: Calypso's mind and body ached with the desire of it.

Sophie was standing at the window when the fog came. In from the sea, where the air was sculpted nightly, mixed on a grey-green palette. Green and grey it swept along the banks of grass and furze. It dredged the ancient moat that circled the Manor like a sorcerer's charm, then fell lazily on to Gerard Winstanley's kitchen garden. The garden dozed in a warm blanket of fog. The very slugs fell limply to the ground. All this time, Sophie watched and could do nothing. Already she felt her head, arms, fingers, weighing upon her, the lids of her eyes. Heaviest of all was the smell… the sweet perfume that nevertheless sent a shiver of revulsion through her, as her head bowed and the bubbling flood rose over all the house, up to the gilded bird that swung the weather round, and drowned it.

PART THREE

CALYPSO DREAMING

22. Transfiguration

Dawn was the slackening of a curtain. The Manor slept through it. The rest of Sweetholm slept. No one knew about the rooks that pitted the ash in the yard, nor the brindled tom that chased them and upset the churn. That noise made Sal stir a little, but her eyes did not open.

Dominic woke first and found himself in Gerard Winstanley's office. It was the stonechat that wakened him, rushing back and forth among the rowan branches. That, and the sun on his closed eyes. It was early morning. The wall clock told him so, but his mind could not take it in. Instead he blinked, and blinked. He was staring at his fingertips. At each knuckle grew a wisp of brown feather.

Will it come to that? he thought, aghast.

He put his hand to his face, fearful of what he might find. With relief he felt the familiar contours of his own nose. His forehead was all skin, his hair all still hair. Only his eyebrows seemed a little longer than before and curled and tapered at the tips. His hearing was sharper, he thought. But perhaps that was only the silence of the place.

The Manor seemed fretful in its breathing. The house was creaking like a ship. Calypso dreamed, somewhere. A few feet away Winstanley was still asleep at his desk, his admonitory finger still pointing heavenward. Calypso's dream had engulfed them all.

Dominic prayed. On his knees he whispered fervent words to the God of Sweetholm and of the universe. God – who hatched the germ that crippled the flesh of the children of Lasithi. God blew healing through him, yes God was merciful. God loved him, he knew. But the love of God might mean anything. What was it like to be loved by a rainbow? Or an idea? Or an infinity of starlit space? Which was most like God's love?

The words got no further than his lips. Dominic realised that his faith was leaving him. His faith, not his belief. God was still there – how could it be otherwise? But Dominic no longer cared to do God's will and felt that for his part God was indifferent. The divorce between them would be friendly, rational and sad.

His legs ached as he stood up. He knew that Sweetholm was unravelling. His understanding of the place had been tantalising, then sudden – like the recognition of a face. Until yesterday, the signs had been ambiguous. Calypso's eyes and fingers, the spectral pilgrimage he occasionally sighted making westwards, the odd events he had made a point of hearing about in the Haven. All this had been tentative. Now Sweetholm was possessed. The demon of the place was active once again and working through Calypso.

Calypso was the key. In any place she would have been dangerous – which was no more than to say that she was wondrous, magical, a sport of nature. Her dreams had power. But on this island, at this time, she was lethal.

Above the door opposite Winstanley's desk the closed-circuit television screen was still switched on. The excitable flicker it gave when Dominic looked at it was his only clue that it was no longer powered by the mains. The screen, as before, was sectioned into six. Dominic remembered Winstanley's prudently chosen vantage points, with their cumulative perspective on the Manor and its approaches. Much good that did against the fog, he thought. Much good it did Gerard Winstanley.

He examined each section of the screen in turn. Top right: no longer a view of the yard, this now showed the seafront at the Haven, looking to the ferry dock. No one to be seen. The sea scudded with mist and shapes inside the mist. Bottom right: Sal was slumped across the kitchen table, two floors below. A wine glass had stained the pine blood-red, soaking into her hair. Top centre was a rocky slope. On the Tor, probably. And there were Harper and Tansy nearby, just beginning to stir. He noted the shape of a fallen rock in the heather, the rank green lichen.

Top left was near total dark. A liquid glint unfolded a corner of the tucked-in darkness and showed Dominic an underground lake and something gliding at its surface. What it was, he could not tell. Bottom left: a face, lit by candles. Deep-creviced cheeks, forehead pitted with age. But nothing could light the black 'O' of its mouth. Its bottom lip gulped out water in a jerking stream.

Bottom centre: here was Calypso herself, in her truckle bed in the room below his feet. She lay in her nightshirt, on top of the thin cover. Although she had been facing the wall, as he looked he saw her turn in sleep. Her sleeping eyes were wide open. At the same time, Dominic had the impression of a change of light just at the edge of the room, as though someone had cast a shadow. He watched, hoping to catch a glimpse of her companion, but saw no one.

Dominic made a decision. He took Winstanley's silver paperknife from his desk and stepped towards the stairwell. For all his stealth, the wrought-iron of Winstanley's spiral staircase vibrated under his feet. As he gripped the rail, he saw how his nails had grown, how they had sharpened and curled, and clicked on the metal like talons. Had that been so when he had awoken? He wasn't sure. Nor did he have time to consider it, for he was already outside Calypso's room.

The room was in the corner of the house. The windows were shuttered, but he could hear the rush and flurry of the air on the two outside walls. Inside, the air was stiflingly still, and saturated with lavender. Calypso lay as he had seen her on the CCTV screen. He glanced at the corner of the ceiling. There was, of course, no camera mounted there.

The room seemed to be flying. The wind was blowing in sunlight, beating the shutters with its powdery fists. The shadows of branches skipped over the shifting cover.

He knelt beside her, making his face level with hers. Calypso's eyes saw nothing. How beautiful she was! More beautiful because of her deformity – yes, that was true. He hardly dared touch her. To cut her flesh, it was unthinkable. His knife dropped to the floor.

Yet the well of dreams must be capped. If he had any purpose left, it was this. To be blessed and damned at the same moment, for the same act, in the same breath. The paradox of it lured him on.

Beside his hand was a fallen pillow. A worm of thought burrowed into his mind. Perhaps, if he were gentle. Perhaps Calypso's life – Sweetholm's enchantment – might be ended mercifully. Without even waking her. He looked at her glistening face with love. But that only made his resolution more secure. He raised the pillow above her face, and gathered all his weight to press it down.

"*Ungh!*"

A blow to the head knocked Dominic sideways. He fell to the floor. His left temple was about to explode, and for a moment he was blind with the sheer pain and surprise of it.

A woman was standing over him. The hem of her long skirt brushed his feet. Blearily, his eyes strayed upward, over acres of *fleurs de lys*, to a belted waist…

Another blow sent him reeling across the floor, away from Calypso's bed. Dominic felt a long wooden club slamming into his skull. He raised his hand to his head and felt it sticky with blood. Rolling over, he looked into the face of his assailant. For a moment he did not recognise her: the face scarcely seemed a human one. The smell of lavender was overpowering.

"Sophie?" he whispered.

"Bastard!"

Dominic scrambled to his feet, slipping in his own blood as he did so. Sophie was coming at him again, a log from the hearth clutched in her hands. Her mouth roared. Dominic knew the voice, that it was as old as Sweetholm. It crackled with age and dust.

"Anathema! Anathema maranatha!"

The curse put despair like a black stone in Dominic's heart. Again the club swung toward him. Dominic just managed to put a chair between him and his attacker, and while Sophie raised herself, he wrenched the door open and flung himself down the stairs at the back of the Manor.

An observer watching from the Tor's slopes might have been surprised by the transformation that now overcame Dominic. Rushing clumsily through the Manor gates he hesitated, uncertain where to go. A glance back at the building showed a pale face at one of the upper windows. At that he turned and fled, headlong towards the foot of the Tor itself. But his arms began to flail and his legs lost their power. Instead of running, he seemed to skim the ground, to be moving almost on tip-toe. His long neck stretched forward. It would be impossible to say at just which moment he ceased to be a man. But it is certain that by the time he was fifty yards beyond the Manor his arms had swarmed with feathers and his long legs were tucked up behind him. And it was a kink-necked bird that finally mounted the air and flew up gracelessly toward the Tor.

★ ★ ★

Davy Jones held his blade up to the sun. A man who took pride in his work, he was gratified to find the edge miraculously sharp: a dangled leaf was bisected with ease. Davy began to whistle, then checked himself as he remembered the gravity of the place and his own function. Instead, he scrutinised his face in the polished flat of the scythe. His beard, shaved off on impulse, lay at his feet in orange caterpillar curls. As a result he looked much younger. His cheeks were pink and flabby with vitality. He smiled and corrected a stray loop of hair.

Last night's vigil had been a long one. The sea had frothed over all the island, until Sweetholm was reduced to one small rock, on which Davy Jones had sat. He had seen the goddess's power at work. He had ridden that power, as on a cloud.

It had been some time – one day at least – since he had heard any movement from the cave beneath his feet. He considered the possibilities. Either Geoff Robinson had fallen unconscious or else he had wandered down to some lower cave and lost his footing. In that case, Davy would not expect to see him again. More likely, though, he had made his way to the ledge overhanging the sea opposite Longholm. If so, might he have had the agility to haul himself back on to the cliff top and freedom? Davy Jones pondered the matter. No, he would not.

Davy lay on the ground, next to the gap between the

rocks where a snaking hole gave access to the cave.

"Mr Robinson? Hello?"

Silence.

"Have you had your fill of the antiquities, Mr Robinson?"

Silence. The shuffle, was it, of sodden feet?

"Because our tour is at an end now. Put your hand in your pocket, Mr Robinson, I shall be asking for gratuities!"

Lithe as the rope he carried, Davy Jones lowered himself through the cave entrance, pulling the scythe after. It clattered against the rock, flashing spikes of daylight into the shadow.

Here comes a candle to light you to bed.

Davy let himself drop. He found he was in water up to his calves. Gradually, he made his way to Brigan's cave. He saw, but only faintly, the glimmering face of the goddess. She wore a coronet of shells. Her hands were pincers, crab and lobster hands. There was no sign of Geoff Robinson. Her choking mouth coughed out water, as though she had nearly drowned.

Davy Jones was overcome. He flung himself before her image and his legs began to tremble. Brigan's voice was speaking: not only in his mind now.

Thou good and faithful servant.

"Yours for ever, Lady," pledged Davy Jones. He set about lighting the candles. Many had been entirely submerged by the water, which continued to flow from Brigan's mouth.

A stone-cold breeze sliced the air as Brigan began her catechism.

Why did you sharpen your blade, Davy Jones?

"To spill the blood of your enemies. To rid Sweetholm of heretics and false priests."

I have stretched out my hand to them. Why did you shave yourself, like a lamb sheared for slaughter?

Davy Jones said nothing. A wild hope rose in his heart.

Had Brigan really guessed his most secret desire? He felt for the scythe at his side.

The time has come to complete yourself. Now you must make yourself perfect.

There was a splash as Davy Jones knelt before her. The blade flashed. A sigh as he swooned into the water. The scythe fell beside him. The candlelight glimmered on the crimson pool.

The taste of my love is a bitter taste, said Brigan of Sweetholm.

23. Longholm

Tansy remembered little, except the night's strange indoor warmth. The Channel all round them and the sky sieving starlight. On almost any other night the Tor would have sucked her life away. Tonight she was comforted. She woke unwillingly, to find Harper shaking her by the arm.

"Look, Tansy!"

"What? What is it?"

Harper was pointing to a large bird making for the Tor from east to west. Its flight was laborious; it was too heavy to soar as a true seabird should.

"A heron," said Harper. "You never see them here. What a beauty!"

They watched the heron pass overhead. As it reached the summit of the Tor, they saw that it was no longer alone. A swarm of white shapes had lifted from the cliff beyond. Gulls – dozens of them – were pouring from the nesting ledges, enraged. They swooped menacingly close. Then one gull launched itself into the heron's body.

The larger bird seemed to shudder. It fell twenty yards then, painfully flapping, gradually hiked itself higher. But by that time more gulls were mobbing it.

"Oh!" cried Tansy. A vicious buffet had shaken the heron from the sky, like a crumb being shaken from a napkin.

Tansy and Harper watched it fall, a gangling feathery mass, on to the scrub below.

They found the bird later, hanging from the fork of an elder branch halfway up the Tor. Its feathers were plucked and gouged, exposing the grey flesh beneath. Its legs were icicles of wax.

"Poor thing!" said Tansy. "Is it quite dead?"

"Quite," Harper confirmed, lifting the head and letting it drop. "Just as well. We'd have had to wring its neck."

Tansy looked over her head, where a couple of gulls were still circling.

"Why did the gulls attack it?"

Harper replied, but with no great conviction, "It's still the nesting season, just. They'll do anything to protect the next generation." He rubbed his nose and added in a more puzzled tone, "Anyway, a heron's got no reason to be out here. Must've got lost somehow in this fog."

They looked out to sea again. Sweetholm was the rim of the world. Beyond, the fog was dark, but not quite silent.

Tansy grabbed his arm. "Harper, I'm frightened. This can't be natural. Why is the fog out there? The island's all bright sun — there's even a wind. There shouldn't be a sea fog, should there?"

Harper opened his mouth to answer.

"Dominic really was right," said Tansy. "I saw it as soon as I woke up. The colours aren't real any more. The flowers, they're too... *bright*. Like a kid's drawing. Even the distances have changed. Look over there, to our house. That's two miles away. But, Harper, I swear I can see my mother feeding the hens in the yard! She's taken off her wedding ring!"

Hilary was even smiling. Each handful of corn was a scattering of molten sun. Tansy blinked away a tear the wind had drawn from her. The miracle of distance did not survive it and she could no longer see her mother. But Harper nodded. "It all comes through Calypso's mind now."

He took her hand, and they continued their ascent. The Tor was not a mountainous climb, but it was a deceptive one, full of tracks that wound to nothing, twists and sudden drops. Beyond the summit, with its small plateau and its whitewashed trig point, the descent was more perilous still. All the time, Tansy's sense of unreality grew until she felt as if she were only dreaming of herself. There she was, scrambling over the dry, dry rocks in the clear, clear air and everything being too much itself, too bright and too hard, except for her and Harper, who grew thinner and less real with every breath. Even the flies, which had persecuted her all summer, now seemed oblivious as she sweated over the Tor's ridges.

Abruptly, the rock ceased. They found themselves on the scrubby patch of shallow land just shy of the cliff. The wind furrowed the grass, rattling twigs of rosemary like coral in the green undersea. Then it skewed off and left them in shelter and sudden silence. Above, small clouds speckled the dragonfly-blue sky.

Tansy's certainty of the evening before had melted in this vibrant light.

"What are you thinking, Harper? You think it's all hopeless, don't you?"

He looked her in the eye. "What do *you* think?"

"Last night I was so sure we could make a difference," said Tansy plaintively. "But today... It's hard to believe in anything on a day like this."

"Then try!" cried Harper. "Try to believe or what hope have you got? The island is enchanted, Calypso's beyond reach, your dad is gone and no one but you is going to get him back. You better make your mind up, Tansy, you better start believing in something, fast."

"I want to!"

"That's not enough!"

Harper stalked off to the cliff edge. Tansy watched him, then crept fearfully to his side, just as a savage wave gouged the rocks below. The spray blinded her, a shimmering abstract of pale and darker lights, and the echoes trapped between them. Her stomach turned. The seals on the sleek black rock of Longholm lounged indifferently. Tansy saw Harper flinch as another wave detonated at their feet and the sea recoiled in frenzy. The spray hovered in the air. Then a devious wind undershot it and moulded the hanging water to make an arch. For an eyeblink they truly saw it there, spanning the sea between Longholm and the cliff at their feet: a bridge of white air. They could almost have set their feet upon it.

"Tansy? Do you see?" said Harper hoarsely.

"Oh, Harper! Look at the seals down there!"

The group of three or four seals watching them from Longholm had swollen, in the last minute, to more than a dozen. Their heads were all lifted towards the strip of rainbow air where a few water drops still refracted the ghost of a path. The heads dropped, as if in disappointment, as it faded.

"They saw it too," said Tansy. "They *knew.*" The colour had drained from her voice. "They're dead men, Harper, they're some awful story from a peat hearth. Let's get away."

They moved from the edge of the cliff. Harper was combing the ground. Just before the nearest ridge lay a stunted trunk of wood, almost hidden by brambles. Tansy crouched to examine it.

"What is it, Tansy?"

Harper squatted beside her, to find her looking at a rope that dangled from the trunk into black space.

For a minute neither of them said anything. The hole stared back.

"You said you wanted to go abseiling," said Tansy.

"Potholing's a different game," said Harper and added with a taut smile, "It's dark down there."

Tansy's reply was drowned by a fresh explosion of water from the rocks behind her. She could hear the foam cling to the cliff face as it receded, fingers clawing every gulley.

"Harper!" she cried. "Where are you going?"

Harper had raised himself. "Just stay close, will you?"

He gripped the rope and tugged at the tree stump. It was firm. Without giving himself time to think better, he lay prone and began to shimmy back into the darkness. Soon, all Tansy could see of him was his face.

"Are you all right?" she called as he disappeared.

"Yes!" came Harper's voice, sounding small and far away. "Wait!"

She waited. Harper did not return. For two minutes she listened to the beating of her heart. Then two minutes more, with the rope lying in her hand.

"Harper! Answer me!"

To go after him was madness. Madness to stay.

And she let herself down, spinning on the rope, and landed in water up to her knees. She was in darkness, except for the light above that haloed her. She called, but it was a chamber in which only the sea's voice carried; and that was everywhere. At last she saw the darkness flicker a little way ahead. Carefully, she moved in that direction, to the Tor's heart.

★ ★ ★

Harper had been drawn too far away to hear Tansy's cries. Beyond the rope, he found a space in which he could easily stand upright. He could not so much as feel the roof above his head and the echoes he started as he waded through the cold water told him he was in a sizeable cave. The water itself surprised him. Wasn't this cave too high for even the highest tide? But then the Channel was notorious.

The light from the hole above dimmed rapidly. Yet he found that he could still make his way forward, that a trace of light grazed the darkness ahead. As he moved towards it, the blackness became still more diffuse. He made out an edge of rock, a shadow, the breath of a further chamber lit feebly from within. He turned a corner and found himself looking out at a world of unspeakable brightness, a bouquet of plastic colours. He was on the ledge overlooking Longholm.

At once a monstrous wave rose from the sea. Its green underbelly was molten glass; it fell and shattered on the headland. Harper had never seen such a wave before, never heard such thunder. Longholm almost vanished in the aftershock, the white spray that chased its own echo up and out of the chasm. The cold made his skin ache. Then the whiteness thickened and shrank. It was bounded by the false cobalt blue of the sky over Longholm, and by Longholm itself. Between them and the ledge curled a bridge of spray and stone. Again the sea was hoisting a phantom out of itself, the memory of the arch that once joined the larger island with its outpost.

This time, though, the arch did not dissolve.

The seals had seen it too. Their heads were lifted high as they sniffed at a new scent. But now Harper did not think they looked like seals at all.

They were not seals and they were not going to stay on Longholm. Whatever congregation dwelt there, it had begun its eastward pilgrimage. The creatures were climbing the impossible bridge towards him. Their eyes were hidden by broad flaps of skin, or cloth, that gleamed black under the unnatural sunlight. Every movement was a mortal effort, but they moved nevertheless, straining against the weight of their own waterless bodies then collapsing forward, each time a few inches higher, to the place where Harper stood.

How many centuries of death were woven on that loom, the shuttle clacking back and forth over that sea's edge? The stories of Longholm were ones that Harper knew. Davy Jones had told them round the Manor fire and watched Calypso's jaw hang in wonder. In that moment, Harper saw John Robinson, he saw the monks of St Brigan's priory, the sailors ruined on the schooner *Jago*. All of them were climbing the arch of spray towards him.

He turned and ran back to find Tansy and the rope.

24. The Iconoclast

Brigan was waiting for Tansy. Or rather Tansy found there the stinking limestone column that Davy Jones had tricked out with fragments of shell and bone. Tansy looked closely. Brigan's face, so far as she could see by the light of the candles, was coarsely worked. A jet of water gulped from her mouth, at heartbeat intervals. Her glaring sockets suggested a skull, though some kind of clay, or painter's mummy – you could not call it skin – was smeared across her cheeks. The effect was made for distance, here where there was none. The arm Tansy recognised, of course, from the beach where she and Harper had found it. And Davy Jones had discovered, or more likely manufactured, a second, which lay across the figure's lap as though it were nursing some exquisite toy. The legs were merely suggested under a skirt of netting that already dragged in the water.

Tansy began to wade around this creation, keeping her eyes always upon it. Strangely, the cruder the idol seemed the more fearful it made her. Something realistic, a tailor's mannequin, would not have frightened her half as much. But this magic made no concession. She couldn't take her eyes off it.

So it was a shock when she rapped her shins on something hard. She cried out in sudden pain. The thing moved – it was floating just below the surface of the knee-deep water.

"Harper!"

She closed her hand upon a length of wood. Lifting it, she found the haft of Davy Jones's scythe. The blade was entangled with Brigan's skirt and cut itself loose as she pulled. Lit by the candles behind her, the polished blade curved away, waning westward.

The metal gleamed on another object in the farther darkness. It was long, splayed and shapeless with cloth. At one end something was sticking out from it, about the size of a football. She moved closer and saw a gill of white flesh open and close. A face smiled back up at her. But the gash in Davy Jones's throat was wider than any smile.

"*Harper!*"

Harper heard her scream as he came running from the sea ledge. At once he saw Brigan and the shrine that had bloomed around her. Brigan's mouth was jittering out gulps of candleflame water, more and more rapidly. Her tongue rang with the race of water sluicing through it.

"There, Tansy! That's what's drawing them all in! Can't you feel the power of it? You've got to destroy that thing!"

But Tansy was not listening. She had raised Davy Jones's scythe. She had, for that moment, seen it all. Brigan's weeping eyes had told her. Of her loneliness she could not speak, for there were no words. She could speak of nothing.

"Tansy, what are you doing?" Harper could hear the rushing of the sea outside the cave. The raw sun shone like arc-light on the walls behind him. There were shadows swaying to and fro in that light. A few more moments and they would be cut off from the cave's exit. "There's no time to think about it! Those ghouls have followed us. They'll be at the rope by now. Do you *want* to die?"

Tansy said, "I want to see…"

The ghosts of Longholm shambled forward over the rock. They were wading through the shallow pools, their clumsy heads lolling with each step. Harper caught the reek of their flesh as the wind curled back through the cave.

"I want to see my dad again," said Tansy. She sounded like a very little girl.

"Your dad? Jesus, Tansy, get a grip!"

"That's why I came here, Harper! If we leave now, I'll *never* get him back," she said hopelessly. "And I want – I do want him. You never knew him. How he could be—"

"Tansy, your dad – he won't be as you expect. He'll be changed…"

You shall have him, Brigan promised, with a gaze that chained her own. *You shall have him back, and all shall be well. Listen! He is coming, quickly!*

Tansy turned and by the candlelight it seemed to Harper that something of Brigan's pale hunger already festered in her cheek. She was staring past Harper, to the farther cave. Dozens of creatures were rasping out air in the chamber beyond, the sad train of Brigan's liegemen. She had led them shimmering through sunlight and fathomless water, and now to this desperate place.

Harper dared not look. The terror he read on Tansy's face was enough. When she dropped the scythe he knew she had seen her father.

★ ★ ★

"*Daddy!*"

By the time they came running, Calypso was already sitting up in bed. Her eyes were saucers. She gripped the sheets like spars from a wreck.

"She's dreaming again."

Sophie was there first. She spoke to Calypso and sobbed and

shook and shook her. To begin with, Calypso responded to none of this. Sophie turned to Sal, hardly able to speak. "She still can't hear me. Hasn't Gerard got through to Plinth yet?"

"The lines are dead."

Sal had woken from deep sleep an hour before. Sophie had shown her the blood on the floor in Calypso's room, but could give only the most disconnected account of what had happened. Sal had dealt with that side of things calmly enough. By the time Winstanley appeared, looking dishevelled in yesterday's clothes, both the log and Sophie's bloodstained skirt were well alight in the hearth below and the floor was scrubbed. To Gerard's bleary enquiries they could suggest only that Dominic must have left the house early, on what project of his own who could guess? But Dominic was not the only absentee. Harper and Tansy were missing too. The phone lines were down and even the shortwave radio conjured nothing but static. Moreover, Calypso's sleep was now punctuated with cries – of Queenie, of Harper, over and again of a bridge. And now this.

Sophie gave herself up to a box of tissues. "I'm to blame," she complained.

"Not you, pet, not you," said Sal.

Sophie stared at her friend. Her voice was cold and unforgiving.

"Where Calypso's concerned, it'll always be me."

★ ★ ★

"*Daddy!*"

It was not Tansy's voice. Harper stared at Brigan. She had lost the adornments with which Davy Jones had besottedly decked her. He saw nothing but a stump of rock, punctured in three places and pumping water. Yet a moment earlier he had heard Calypso calling from that rock.

Tansy was trying to stand, but the current buffeted and swayed her. Harper launched himself forward.

"Tansy, reach my hand…"

But something else had been summoned to the water's surface and now Harper saw it. At first it seemed no more than the foaming of a wave. But this wave had claws, five of them. It had claws and skin, a scaly hide that ran its length and glistened as it touched the air. A moment later he saw the head as well – and a crocodile's long tail whipping into the stump of rock. The rock cracked like an egg shell.

Then came chaos. Harper heard splinters of stone fly past him and shatter in the darkness. His ears were an agony of water. Something soft and horribly strong had wrapped itself about his legs and was dragging him down, down…

Tansy heard Harper's voice, but his words – if they meant anything – were drowned by the percussion of Brigan's tongue upon the roof of the world, her vast, despairing roar. Tansy was spinning like a leaf on a meltwater stream. A meteor of blue light shot past – the cave's upper entrance. She was aware that she was grabbing for the rope; that it had slithered numbly through her hands; that she had missed it. She and Harper were being pulled out through the cave, and in the grip of this ebb tide she was powerless, jostled in a rout of limbs, of faces soft as tissue. Long fingers tentacled the water, dabbed and stung her flesh. Out and over the bridge from Longholm the phantoms slipped – and there the atomising laser sun astonished them. Each ghost became a rainbow matrix of light, became nothing. The bridge itself, that confection of memory, buckled under the weight of water flowing from the cave and fell.

Tansy and Harper fetched up on the ledge. A creature stood beside them, the stream breaking over it as if it were a rock. Darkness had made its blinking pink-white eyes sandblind. Its face was scabrous and in its midst two broad lips were pushed into an unnatural pout. Tansy heard Harper speak a name.

"Joe? Is it you?" There was wonder in his voice, as well as fear. "Did you destroy the sanctum? Did Calypso call you?"

But the creature had turned back into the torrent and was gone.

For a long time they were too tired to move. A little behind them, in the cave mouth, lay Geoff Robinson. One hand was being knocked rhythmically forward by what was left of the current, but as it lessened the hand grew still. A fine lace of blood had spread from the back of Geoff's head. When Tansy let herself look at Harper, she found he too was staring at the wound.

"Is he alive?" she asked. She felt detached from her own words. Someone else was speaking them.

"I think so. I saw his chest move. I ought to get help, Tansy."

"You'll not leave me?" she said in alarm. "Not after all this?"

Harper tried to raise himself and winced. "No, I'll not leave. I think my ankle's bust, I'd never make it up the rope."

"Good," said Tansy.

Harper grimaced. "You're a good climber, Tansy. You'll have to go."

★ ★ ★

Sal had found the doll on the floor by now. "Poor Queenie. Calypso's ripped her back quite open. The seam's almost undone."

"I'll sew it," said Sophie absently. She passed the doll into her daughter's hand. "Look, Calypso, who's come to see you!"

Calypso eyed the doll squintways. The doll's face smiled back between florid cheeks.

"He served you right," Calypso said sternly and put Queenie aside. Then she looked up at her mother. Her face was bright. "Mummy, you should have seen him! He saved us all."

Sal and Sophie exchanged glances, almost afraid to show the hope they felt. Minutes earlier, Calypso had seemed as deeply lost in sleep as ever. Yet here she was, sitting up in bed and spinning stories as if the whole world were nothing but a tapestry of her own imagining. Sal put on her bright, questioning face.

"Who did, darling? Tell me about your dream."

"No dream!" insisted Calypso. "This was real! I don't dream, ever!"

"No?"

After a minute Calypso added, "I think he'd been waiting to do it, too, ever such a long time."

"Who do you mean?"

"Daddy! Only he's a strange man now." Calypso warmed to the thought. "You should see him. He can't help being ugly, Mummy, but inside he's just beautiful. I should have dreamed about him long ago. I'm sure he wanted me to."

Sophie followed little of this. But her gift lay in grasping what was essential. She kissed Calypso on the forehead. She kissed her tenderly on the palm of each hand. "Joe loved you, even though he never saw you. He called you his Lucky Charm."

"That's right," said Calypso complacently. "I am."

And, pulling the bedclothes around her neck, she fell asleep soundly.

The women returned to the smoking fire in the room below. A driftwood log was turning mildly to ashes. No one was there but Winstanley, twiddling dials. He looked up and called excitedly, "I just raised Plinth!"

"How much does she understand?" Sal asked Sophie. She looked exhausted, her skin sallow.

"Nothing, of course." Staring at the ash, Sophie traced the C of her daughter's name with the end of a poker. Of course a four-year-old could not control her own dreams. No one could.

From her pocket she took a metal box, large enough for a

coin or a medal. Inside was a disc of callused skin. It was brittle now and white with salt. Outside the window, the sky's picturebook brightness had leached away, leaving it soft and water-blue. A breeze was ruffling the high clouds.

Then she added wonderingly, "Everything! She understands it all."

At that moment Tansy lifted the back door latch. Smiling, she stumbled into the room among them. Her hair was lank and wet. She looked as if she had been washed up with the tide and was shivering so that she could hardly speak.

"Harper and my dad," she stammered, still smiling. "They're injured, both of them. By the Tor. I think you'd better call up Plinth and get some help."

APOCRYPHA

Autumn on Sweetholm is a time of withdrawal. At the end of October the daily ferry shuts down. After that, the only traffic is a weekly shunting of supplies, along with such passengers as find it necessary to make the trip in either direction, and they are few. Among the villagers of the Haven the loss of the summer trade is regretted, but they are far from inconsolable. With the lengthening nights, Sweetholm reverts to its own. The voices in the Haven Inn become a little louder, the jokes a little bawdier. The November gales are ripping the sea like paper and the storm lanterns are swinging, and the time has come for the telling of stories.

In the Haven the account of what happened on the Tor that day soon lost the jagged quality of fact. Adam Fagan, the harbour master, would describe how Geoff Robinson had killed Davy Jones in a fight over a woman, and had escaped punishment only by buying off the mainland police. No one contradicted him. Others, remembering the convulsions of the weather, murmured ominously against the rashness of meddling with Nature. Some even latched on to Calypso as the cause of it all. The word 'witch' began to be mentioned.

"I always said her eyes could see straight through you."

"She did for that priest, you know. Only they can't prove anything."

The things that were being whispered made life on Sweetholm intolerable to Sophie and Calypso. They left the island shortly afterwards, with no word as to their destination.

Gerard Winstanley was deeply shaken by the whole ordeal. He even described it as a kind of baptism. He began to despise his former life and the ease with which he had been able to purchase a sense of virtue. He resolved to build himself again – from deeper and from further back. He sold his shares and started a fund to cure the Red Leprosy, then at its height. The Dominic Fowey Trust, despite hooking Science to the Money Engine, was eventually successful in finding a treatment for the disease. Thus, Winstanley saved the lives of hundreds and rescued thousands more from the crippling indignities of the illness. The thought brought him happiness and a wholesome kind of pride. By that time, however, the work of the Asklepians was more urgently required elsewhere.

One Saturday in late November a small group gathered at the ferry dock. The boat was loading.

"Goodbye," said Harper.

"Goodbye."

"Goodbye."

Tansy kissed him. Geoff had already parked the car on the narrow ferry deck.

"Goodbye."

Extraordinary things happen every day, thought Tansy. Here she was leaving Sweetholm – and her mother – to go back to Bristol. And it all felt as inevitable as breathing. "Goodbye, Mum. I'll ring you when we get home. Let you know we're safe."

"Be sure you do."

Winstanley, Sal and some of the others from the Manor had come too. Hilary had seen a good deal of them in recent weeks.

During Geoff's recovery Sal, in particular, had been an indispensable friend.

Geoff's convalescence had been steady. He was a biddable patient and with the care of Hilary and Tansy his head injury had soon healed. Only the rash on his arm left a permanent mark, a glossy scar about the size of a playing card, but this soon ceased to pain him. He began to eat more and to take exercise – at first within the narrow grounds of Crusoe's Castle. Each morning he beat its bounds in what quickly became a superstitious ritual. Later he ventured to the gun battery and even the beach. As his body recovered, however, he grew more anxious to leave the island. The sight and smell of the sea disgusted him and there was no escaping either on Sweetholm. "She's not dead," he would say sometimes, looking up at the Tor, "only sleeping." He was a martyr, too, to nightmares of the most distressing kind.

Hilary took Tansy in one of her embraces that was almost a whisper. "It won't be for long."

"I know that, Mum," replied Tansy, looking at her steadily. By a series of steps as formal as a dance, her parents were separating. There would be no reunion.

"Just till the lawyers have sorted out Uncle John's affairs. And then I may come back to Bristol. Perhaps you'll join me here."

"I know – we've said all this. I've missed a lot of school. We'll have to see."

"I have high hopes." Hilary let her go, but still seemed as if there were more she wished to say. "I've not always been the perfect mother," she added in the end.

"I like you the way you are, Mum," smiled Tansy.

"When I should have been the one star in your small sky you could steer by."

"I'll steer by my own lights," said Tansy, glancing around anxiously for Harper. She did not want him to see Hilary being sentimental.

"That's what I'm saying. Now you're growing up, we have a chance to get to know each other, don't we? I'll be a better friend to you than I was a mother."

"Tide's on the turn," warned the skipper. "All aboard who's going aboard."

Tansy looked round to say her last goodbye to Harper. But Harper had already left. She spied him on the inland road, climbing the hill to the moor and already hardly more than a wisp of colour. He turned and waved once, as if feeling her eyes upon him, then went on climbing. Tansy shrugged, making allowances for an Aquarian child, and assured herself that she would see him soon enough. The wind was making her eyes water. Then Geoff honked and she found the skipper waiting, rope in hand, ready to cast off. She picked up her bag and, with only the faintest misgiving, embarked on the ferry back to Britain.

In the years that followed, Harper continued to look for news of Sophie and Calypso, news he felt sure would come. He heard of many incidents that might have borne Calypso's mark: miracles, infestations, prodigious births. But such events were becoming commonplace as Harper grew to manhood. When he reached the age of military service, he chose instead to join the Order of Asklepius in a village east of Mosul, working as a nurse. There the malady known as Ishtar's Curse was making itself felt in a new and virulent form. He cooked food, changed dressings and burned the clothes of those who had died.

Only once did he feel confident that he had caught a glimpse of Calypso. In what the digital news service described as a fatal mixture of freak weather conditions and mass hysteria, some twenty people had been found dead on a small West Indian island, at the tail of the Leeward chain. Even in an area subject to tropical storms, the one that had all but wiped out the coastal village of Chantilly was exceptional, both for its violence and for its very local nature. The neighbouring settlements had been quite unaffected.

Some months earlier, the provincial government had been alarmed by reports of the revival of a voodoo cult. Cattle had begun to sicken. There was talk of unshriven ghosts wandering the village at night, zombies who drank the blood of goats and chickens. All this coincided with the arrival in Chantilly of a young girl, dubbed by the islanders "La Fille qui Rêve." Stories soon spread of her extraordinary powers of healing and foreknowledge. The farmhouse on the outskirts of the village where she lived with her mother became a place of virtual siege.

When the local priest denounced her mother in church, the girl, who was there to hear it, fell at once into a fit and was carried home on a stretcher. The congregation was jubilant at first, believing that the priest had cast out a devil. The following day, however, his body was discovered at the bottom of a ravine. It had been mutilated by a small, voracious carnivore. That same night the storm came and in its frenzy washed Chantilly out to sea. Among the bodies later recovered, neither the girl's nor her mother's was to be found.

Harper downloaded the file. The island, the age of the girl and several other details (which Harper made it his business to discover) all fitted with what he knew of Calypso. But his work left him little time to take matters further. Extreme weather and superstitious murder were becoming ever more common. The evidence was vague, ambiguous. The story's crisis might have many explanations, he saw, without resort to the supernatural.

And this time there were no survivors left to speak of it.